For whoever this may reach, I pray it helps to heal you.

❚

Present day:

Truth be told, I didn't know what it meant. Any of it.

I woke up that morning, and I must have come to some sort of realisation. I realised, I was painting over the feelings I so strongly felt with lies I kept feeding myself. A lot of questions crossed my mind. What did I do to deserve it? Who did I hurt? Why me? I couldn't help but blame myself, but no matter how hard I tried, I was blind to the faults of my own soul. I didn't want it to be a blame game; but it was what it was becoming. And I had to stop. But if I wanted to stop, then I had to first start with asking the important questions. You know? Like, what is this feeling? Why might I be feeling this way? What's making me feel so deeply about something I can't even find the words to express?

Pause.

"I can't keep doing it like this. I'll drive myself insane" I muttered to myself. I sighed.

I can't be the only one feeling this way. There's gotta be some explanation. I've ignored it for weeks, but this feeling won't budge. I don't want to turn numb, because that won't help. And I also, just don't want to turn. I don't want to change. I like myself as me; even with all the faults. But I know, as scary as it seems right now, this thing, these emotions I'm feeling? It'll change me. I'm not willing to picture what it'll be like - you know? The new me. But it's something I'll have to work towards.

Okay, focus.

So here I am; doing what I probably should have done when I first realised that I didn't feel normal. Here I am, and here's my attempt to do what we all try so hard to avoid, what I've tried so hard to avoid. Here's my attempt to tread through my mind.

14th October 2013

"Smart" Hawa said, "I mean, not many people can explain it without it feeling forced."

I didn't think much of it, I mean she only asked for my advice, and one thing I've always been proud of - is my ability to be honest. I don't believe in beating around the bush, or whatever they call it nowadays - if you care about someone, you'll be honest, even if it means it'll hurt them. I mean, it might hurt them in the short term, but you might have helped them out for the long term, and what can be better than that, right?

"It's okay, just promise me you'll actually take my advice this time?" I spoke, looking at her and trying to catch that look she does when whatever I say just goes right through her and she does the opposite anyways. I guess, this situation, was a little more serious, but I was hoping she'd listen.

"Okay, okay. I'll tell him." Hawa spoke with little faith in herself and the words she had just uttered.

She had just gotten her heartbroken by the one she thought she'd marry, and I don't blame her for wanting to give him another chance. Young love and all that malarky. I guess, being as Hawa as she is, for her it was more so accepting that her choice wasn't right for her after all. But I guess, that's the thing right? Do we ever, truly know, what our actual choice is? I mean, we know what we want at times, but is it entirely what we know what we'll need for as long as we live?

"I need to stop this." I muttered to myself.
Hawa looked at me confused. "Stop what?" she asked curiously.

Damn, I didn't realise I said that out loud.

Truth is, I didn't know what had gotten into me, I was all of a sudden, feeling very weird. *Weird.* That's one way of describing it.

"Oh nothing, I just stayed up late last night and I'm just tired." I replied as fast as I could - as to not make it look like I actually had to think of an answer.

What was I trying to cover up after all? The night couldn't have been as bad as I was making it out to be, in my mind, right?

"Hm, okay, but you can talk to me okay?" She said, knowing full well I'd just laugh it off and avoid the topic anyways.

How would I even begin talking about this? It came to me at times when I least expected it. You'd think, at times when you're distracted with other things, it wouldn't affect you as much right? But you're back to feeling the same darkness that kept you awake all night. The same darkness, you had now becoming tired of fighting. The same darkness you became afraid of becoming. How would I even find the confidence to say these words out loud? What would I say? That I'm scared of my mind and I don't know how to stop? If I couldn't accept it as it was myself, I didn't expect others to do so. Even if it meant, I had to hide it from my own best friend. So be it.

"Yeah, silly, I know that. I told you I'm just tired." I said, making a silly face in the process so as to sound more convincing in my lie.

Lying was almost becoming a chore, and I'm not sure how long I could keep it up.

Saved by the bell, or does that sound too cliche? Eh, who cares.

It was time for class, and we had the most dreaded class you can imagine. Yeah, you got it right. We had Maths. What did I even think choosing this as an A-Level? You'd think someone would have had enough of it at GCSE, but A-Level, come on Dunya, what were you thinking?! We sat at the back of the class as always; still it didn't stop the teacher from picking on us. She must have known we were trying to blend in with the clever ones and somehow make it look like we understood. I guess the nodding didn't help and we might have overdone it at times.

"What's that?" Hena nudged me, pointing towards my sleeve.

"What's what?" I said, trying my best not to sound annoyed by her weird question, or even her existence. *Yeah, I just said that.*

You see, Hena was the type to interrogate you about things that did not concern her. In other words, she was as nosey as they come.

"Poking your nose in something that doesn't concern you again, I see?" Hawa shot back, trying her best to save me from whatever it was.

I guess she knew, but we were both too scared or even frightened to admit that I could do that to myself.

I stretched the sleeves of my blouse over my hands and hoped. Hoped that perhaps she might think she was mistaken. But, how long was I going to get away with this?

And here it comes. The first thread I'm pulling from this mind of mine.

4th October 2013

It was the early hours of Friday morning. And I can't believe I made it the entire night. There was this feeling I couldn't quite get myself to understand. I felt defeated, as though something had come and taken away all the happiness I've been feeling lately. I felt a sudden burden on my chest. It all just felt so heavy. I was taking deep breaths as though it would help. And it did. Up until the point, it just didn't. It wasn't enough. Everything within me was screaming 'PANIC' and I soon began to cry, not being able to control the way I was breathing or even crying.

It lasted a few minutes. My breathing was getting better. I'd stopped crying as much. But my mind hadn't stopped. What was it? Why was I not getting the rest I so desperately wanted from it?

I looked at my skin. And I pinched it. So as to make sure, I'm still awake right? This isn't some kind of weird dream? I guess, I wouldn't want to go into much detail as to scare you away or perhaps myself. But, it got the point where I felt as though I needed to find things to prove to myself that I was still here. And that I was feeling things other than what my mind had dictated. That I was feeling physical pain, as much as mental. I had to prove it to myself, and my mind. I had gotten it drilled into me, by my own hands, that I had to do it. That I had to inflict this physical pain, if it meant I wanted to accept the mental pain too. And I guess, that's where it all started. That one night changed me, into the me I am today.

7

I guess that the one thing the occurrence with Hena taught me, was that no matter how hard I tried to hide things from others, or even myself, it wouldn't make it any less real. Just because, I am not yet in a position to accept that I am feeling a certain way - it does not mean that I don't. You cannot talk yourself into becoming something that you know you're not. It just doesn't make sense. So I had to accept it. And for me to accept it, I had to acknowledge that it wasn't normal. That I wasn't normal. And none of what I was feeling, was normal.

14th October 2012:

"Snap out of it, will you?" Hena spoke.

I was just about to snap back when I realised, it wasn't me she was talking to, but why did it feel like it was a dig at me?

"Dunya, you can answer this question! Explain how Sofia got to this conclusion?" Miss asked.

As any one of us would do in this situation, I looked around, until my eyes met the one trying to mouth the answer to me. I couldn't make it out from the way she was trying to mouth it - but I knew that I had to give an answer. All eyes were on me. And my eyes were too busy squinting. Time was ticking. I had to speak. Come on. S p e a k dunya, speak.

"Erm, she got the answer by working it out?" I shot back with a confused smirk on my face.

I could feel my cheeks beginning to warm up, knowing full well, I just embarrassed myself.

"Great answer Dunya!" Hawa whispered, as she tried so hard not to fall into a pit of laughter.

"Riiiiight, moving on then.. Dunya please pay attention." Miss spoke as she tried not to focus on the embarrassment I just caused myself.

"I know what I'm doing after this Hawa. Can't take it no more." I whispered to her.

I could not take another second of embarrassment - even if it meant I caused it to myself by even choosing Maths in the first place.

"I'm with you sis." She said winking and too excited to even explain.

So when the bell had gone, we made our way down to the head of college. It was one of those situations where you didn't want to speak so you hoped the other one would. It would happen this way, every single time. We would always end up leaving the office without barely entering. But this time, it was different. I was feeling courageous, which was weird, especially for me.

I knocked on the door and waited. No answer.

"Erm maybe she's busy?" Hawa said, hoping not to get into trouble.

I knocked again.

"Yes? How may I help you?" Miss Smith said as she appeared at the door.

She was quite scary; if that's one way of describing her. She had this intimidating vibe, as though, no matter what you said, she would turn it and make it seem like you're in the wrong. Or maybe, I was judging too early, and that can never be good, right?

"Er.." Hawa was stumbling. This can never be good.

"Well, Miss, we were hoping we can talk about our options." First term in, and we were already lacking, this can't look good.

"Sure, you've got 60 seconds, go ahead." Miss spoke, looking sternly at her watch.

"Well, when we were in school we really enjoyed Maths and thought that perhaps we would enjoy it at A-Level too.."

"Errr, Dunya what are you sayi-" Hawa tried saving the moment.

I was quick to interrupt and carry on.

".. But you see the thing is, maths doesn't really seem like a subject that would aid us in our future careers. We just don't feel like we fit in with the class and it's far too confusing and difficult to grasp. So perhaps.. we could drop it?"

At this point, Hawa was standing timidly with one hand placed over her face as though she could not bare to see me embarrassing myself any more today.

"You are aware it's only October and you've only studied it for a month?" Miss spoke, with a little disappointment starting to become apparent.

"Yes.. but what's the point in giving ourselves even more stress when we can just drop it now and focus on other subjects?" I sighed.

"I'll have to get back to you.. Now go, you'll be late for class." She said, pointing towards the corridor.

Silence surrounded us for a good second, until we were in the clear, and that's when the giggles began.

"I cannot believe you just did that." Hawa said, looking at me all surprised.

"I honestly don't know what got into me Hawa." *I really didn't.*

"You know we have your favourite lesson now.." she said, reminding me that was enough excitement for today.

"Erm, not sure there's such a thing? But you carry on, I'm just gonna go to the bathroom." I hurried in the opposite direction.

"Be quick, don't leave me with Zara for long please."

I had to go. I could feel myself becoming a little less courageous, and more.. panicky?

I had to find a space to control my breathing. It was happening. Again. And this time, in a place somewhere other than my bedroom. I didn't know what to do. How to control it. But I knew, I probably just had to let it out. I placed my hands over my mouth, and cried. Cried all the tears I had to cry. Although, I had no idea where all this pain was seeping in from. Why was I feeling like this? Not soon enough, I began to start to stabilise my breathing. I had to stop this. Why wasn't I in control? What was happening?

I was quiet the rest of that day. I didn't have much to say. Or perhaps, I didn't know how to say it. But I just lied again and again when Hawa asked me if I was okay. I just didn't want to make myself think of that again. At least not on purpose.

The evening had come around sooner than expected that day. I didn't want it to, but it did. A part of me was looking forward to the silence of the night, but another part of me, was hoping, that somehow, I wasn't awake to witness it. Even though the nights were quiet, and a time of silence, a time when everyone lays fast asleep - for me it was starting to become a time where my mind began to have this hold over me and everything I didn't know I was even capable of feeling.

I decided I had to do something a little different that night. I wanted to be on my own. But I also knew, I didn't want to feel that panic again. I surrounded myself with family, with what felt like to be the first time in a while. And that's when the thought entered my mind. Almost as though, you've been searching for something for a while, and then it clicks. It was one of those moments for me. At times, it brings me shame that it had to be this way for me to turn back to Allah, but it was necessary, if it meant I wanted to heal. If it meant I wanted some sort of peace.

That night, I saw my mother praying. I saw the way she brought her hands up in front of her, and the way she so delicately placed her thoughts in little whispers, as though, she was almost certain that even though her voice didn't leave the room, it reached the seven heavens. It's as though she was certain that Allah was listening. It felt nice. I wanted that. I wanted to pray. I wouldn't have considered myself 'religious' at that point of my life, or even 'close to God'. I prayed at times, and I fasted during Ramadan. But I didn't reach to Allah for answers when things didn't seem to go my way. It's like I didn't really have a spiritual purpose. And perhaps, the fact I was feeling this way, was Allah telling me that, I do have a purpose. I just have to try harder to find it, so that when I do, everything will make sense.

I knew that if I was to go into it, with everything I had, I would burn myself out spiritually. I didn't want that. I wanted to be consistent; but I also wanted it to last. I didn't want this calling to go so fast. I wanted to accept it and remain there. In other words? *I was willing to help find myself again, if only I don't get lost again.*

I remember that night clearly. I remember the way I dragged my feet to that prayer mat. I remember sitting there for a while. I didn't know what to say. I just thought of how distant I was from God, but at the same time, He called me towards Him when He knew I needed Him most. I felt.. unfaithful. As my thoughts carried me away to the pits of guilt; my tears fell. It hurt, and it's as though I could feel the pain my soul felt in my chest. It was like a burden. Almost like someone's placing a rock on your chest and constantly taking it off - you find it hard to breathe but at the same time, you experience relief. And just like that - even though it hurt - to bare it all, and to cry all the tears I had to cry, it felt.. peaceful. Almost like this is the home my soul had been searching for. I didn't say a word. Yet it felt like, someone had genuinely listened to the pain and I felt comfort. I remember - I didn't want to leave the prayer mat that night. I stayed, as long as my eyes allowed me to.

I opened my Qur'an that night, after what seemed like a while. I kept reading over the same verse, over and over again. It said:

$$\text{فَإِنَّ مَعَ الْعُسْرِ يُسْرًا}$$

Indeed, there is ease with hardship. [Qur'an 94:5]

I read over it. Again and again. It was as though Allah was reassuring me through this repetition. It was as though, He was telling me, ease will come. Parts of me felt guilt. Guilt for becoming distant from Allah in the first place, but other parts of my heart? Felt as though they were being reassured. And not just by anyone, but the Creator of this heart. The Ultimate healer of broken hearts: Allah.

2

Present day:

It's strange isn't it? That even when we move past a certain stage in our lives, we assume that we won't ever have to go back there. We won't have to go back to feeling that way again. In all honesty, doing this, and writing this down, has got me feeling those feelings again. I know that if I was to perhaps feel this way a few months ago, I would panic and allow myself to go down the same route that I've always tried so hard to get out of.

However, looking at it now, and feeling those same emotions has allowed me to to understand something really important. I guess I've learnt to understand that even though we move past certain things in our lives, things that we found really difficult, it does not mean that we won't come across them again. It's kind of like meeting people, who you thought you'd never see again. But it happens, it always does. However, if you tell yourself that this trip down memory lane will only make you feel a certain negative feeling; you're bound to allow it to have that control over your emotions. In most situations, you don't feel that exact way again. It's like, you might feel the same panic, you might feel the same negative thoughts, but the way you deal with them would be much different. And the reason being, is because you've been through it once. You've gotten through the hardest bit. You know how people always say that the first time for anything is always a challenge? It's like that. You've fought that emptiness, you've stayed awake past midnight trying to tame your thoughts. You've dealt with the panic attacks, and yet, you've survived.

You've gotten through the hardest days of your life til date, so if you can do that once, then what's not to say you can't do it again? Right? In a way, another thing that reassures me is that I remind myself that Allah is sending me this as a reminder of all the strength that lives within me; all the

15

strength that I overlook sometimes. I tell myself I'm not going to get through something, and that's when Allah takes it into His hands to remind me: I can do this, not just once, but several times; and however many times after that.

So, here's that strength that I so bravely speak of, and here's my attempt to thread through the second part of my mind.

21st October 2012:

A week had gone by, and in all honesty, I wasn't feeling much different. I had somewhere I could finally call home. My prayer mat. But, my mind was constantly at war with my heart, and I didn't know how to control it. I knew that at times, I had to just let it play out the way it needed to. I knew that, if I wanted to cry, I just had to cry. If I was panicking, I had to let myself panic until I just didn't. I know - it wasn't a healthy way of dealing with it, but it worked in those moments you know?

I knew from the moment I started praying, that I perhaps shouldn't feel entitled to a miracle. My Lord had been calling me towards Him for so long and yet I ignored His calls, and sought happiness in places that just drained me of the little happiness I did have. It's true what they say: the more you seek from this world, the more you'll want. It's like you become so focused on one thing; on one goal, and you become so immune to believing that the dunya has all the answers, that you forget that this is not the case. And it's only until the dunya takes all that you give it, and doesn't return it: that you realise, it simply is just an endless cycle of giving and not receiving. It's like, we can give our all to a person, or to a thing, and it'll lead to attachment. We'll feel happy in the moments leading up the attachment, we'll feel as though we've conquered it all, and we have truly won. When in reality.. we have only begun to lose.. We've begun to lose what our souls have been trying to get us to do for so long. We've begun to lose that little voice taking us to Allah, taking us towards that which will matter in the aftermath of this temporary state. But, all is not lost just yet right? Which is why, Allah allows us to have a second chance. Not even second.. third, fourth, or however many chances it takes for us to realise that the more we chase after the dunya, the more our souls will part from the right path.

Anyways, there I went again, off on a tangent. I seem to be doing that a lot lately.

It was the first time I was seeing Hawa since after the holidays. I was so hell bent on making excuses not to meet up in the holidays just because I knew she'd want to get in my space. Is that bad? I mean, it's strange. It's so strange, because even though at times I felt so lonely, I craved human affection and company, at the same time, I knew its not what I needed and I was only craving it out of loneliness, and in a way that made me feel... selfish? I almost felt like, this was my battle to fight and I couldn't let this pain touch her, or anyone else. Hence, why I kept it all in, until the point I just couldn't.

"Hey stranger." Hawa spoke as she reached in for a hug.

"EW, get off me!" I said, giggling.

I loved making it awkward for her, especially when others were around (Don't ask why, is it a girly thing or am I just strange? Wait don't answer that).

It was 8:10AM and we were one of the first ones in as usual. She didn't really have a choice as her father dropped her off to school; however, I just loved being extra cautious and being at school way earlier than even expected of me.

"So.." she said, eyes drawing in towards my arm and the feeling of seriousness surrounding the air.

"How have you been..?" she asked.

I knew I had to lie, but I felt like she was also getting fed up of my lies you know? It felt like she was being patient, because she knew it wasn't easy, but she must have also felt as though I was pushing her away - because I felt like I was too. I felt distant from everyone, not just her.
I sighed. I looked at her. She was looking at me with those understanding kind of eyes - as though she kinda knew I would lie, but whatever I chose to say in that moment, she'd be okay with it. She really was the sister I never had.

"I started praying again." I spoke, as I looked up from my hands and looked at her. She smiled, as she let me continue.

"It felt nice. It felt like, I didn't even have to say anything, and yet I felt so.."

"Understood?" She said as I was struggling to find the words (as usual).

"Yeah, exactly that. Like, I know with you, I can tell you it, but it's hard to just.." And in that moment I felt a tear roll down my cheeks. I don't think I can do this, not right now. It's too soon.

"It's okay," she said as she came in for a hug and gave me a tissue.

"You don't have to.. it's okay.." she continued.

"Anyways, take this tissue and clean your snot before someone sets eyes on you." She said, trying so hard to smirk in the process and making me scoff out a little laughter.

I took a few minutes to calm myself down, as Hawa sat there, minding her own and doing her work. She was always on top of her revision - more so than me.

"So, last weekend, I went to my cousin's house, and I kind of had a little bit of a "I want to run away" moment." Hawa said, almost laughing in the process, as she finished off the sentence she was writing.

"No way!! Tell me more." I said, eager to know what she had been up to, and who annoyed her now. She was one of those people that would be patient with you; very patient.. unless you really did something to get her cross and she would not let you change her mood.

"So, my cousin sister was there.." She said rolling her eyes.
"You know, the one that always copies what I do?"

I couldn't help but laugh, she was so extra at times and she knew it too.

"She just really annoyed me, and I ended up saying something and my mum told ME, can you believe it! She told ME to apologise."

I was laughing a lot at this point.

"Yeah yeah I'm glad my pain makes you laugh." She said sternly, as a smirk grew on her face.

"You know.." I began to speak.

"Are you about to lecture me? Because I am so NOT here for it." She said, as she pretended to continue writing.

"No serious, Hawa, listen." I said, taking her pen from her hand.

"You know, my mum always says to me that it's better to remain quiet when you're right, than to speak. Purely because if you speak, you allow others to think many things about you. And living in the community that we do, it's common that, even when we don't say anything - they make it into a big deal. But, being quiet when someone is trying to taunt you, has a whole other kind of peace attached to it. It's like you know you haven't done anything, it's on them. But rather, you're choosing to be quiet because the knower of everyone's doings, knows the truth and justice will be served. And what could be better than knowing that, right?"

"You are EXACTLY like my Mum." Hawa said, as she laughed a little.

"I honestly get where you're coming from 100%, but I also feel like the more you let people get away with saying and doing what they wish - the more they do so, just because they know they can." She looked at me.

"Yeah, but the minute you give them the satisfaction of a response, it tells them that it really triggers you and it makes them feel good about themselves. It feeds their egos, and they think, if they can get a reaction out of you - why wouldn't they do it again? More so, in front of others?"

"Okay, okay. I get you." She said, desperately trying to change the topic, as this was something we had such different beliefs on, but both tried so hard to lecture each other on.

The truth is, I also knew where she was coming from. And I admired her for her resilience and strength. It's like, most times, I get told, "dunya you're too kind". I mean, I didn't think much of it at first, like, isn't this how everyone is meant to be? I just know that from everything my mum has told me and all that I have witnessed up until this point: that even though you're kind, people will take advantage of that. But, it's like, I don't know no other way to just be? It's become so immune to think a certain way, or react a certain way to the negativity received from others that I just be myself. No pretences. No fake-ness. Just me. I just be kind. I either deflect their negativity with a smile or just try my best to look past it. Lately though, it's become a bit of a chore to ignore it. I feel like every time I choose to ignore something negative said to me - I'm just making it worse for myself. I keep letting myself believe that it's not worthy of acknowledging in the moment, but then my mind only goes and pick points every little detail, later on, when sleep seems to escape from me. I stay awake, wondering what I could have done wrong or what was it on my behalf that allowed that person to have such a negative reaction to me? It always came down to this blame game, and it just seemed like the blame has been mine. And just mine. How do I stop it? How do I-?

"Earth to Dunya!!!" Hawa said, waving a letter in front of my face.

"Yes?" I spoke, almost sounded relieved, but also strangely annoyed that she stopped me in my thinking tracks.

"What's that letter?" I asked intrigued as to why she seemed so excited about it.

"Oh.. this? Nothing much.. just you know.. a university offer.." she said starting off looking down and then slowly raising her eyes towards me, as though she was dying to jump from joy

"HAWA!" Oops, that was a bit loud.

3

Present day:

One thing that I still don't understand to this day, is how people can say that just because you're depressed or you have a mental illness - you're far from God. I know that with what I've been through, and what I've told you so far, that there might be two ways this book will be taken. One, that might be that it doesn't make sense - how can something you don't know have such a negative control over you? Second, the person that might understand, exactly where I'm writing this from, because you have also been through it. Perhaps, you may be reading this in hope that you can get some answers. Some answers about why you feel this way and how it is that you should cope. I'm hoping that I can help with the latter. But I'm also hoping that I bring to light that mental health in the Muslim community is something that is taken lightly - yet it shouldn't be.

Truth be told, I'm sick of this blame game. Telling someone, that they are "obviously going to be depressed if they carry out sins" or that they "must not pray to God if they're that anxious". I promise you, if anything, its these people with the mental illnesses that try that little harder to achieve some closeness to God, because time and time again, they've come across societal expectations and opinions, and it's almost claustrophobic. How is it that when someone is going through a physical illness - we don't expect them to explain their relationship with God, because we know that it is not down to that, yet when it comes to a mental illness, we automatically assume that it's got to be down to that. That they must be going through it because they hardly have a relationship with God. I feel like, there's not much strength in criticising others. In fact, I don't think there's any strength in you as a person if you feel the need to criticise someone and their relationship with God, just on the basis of what they tell you they feel.

There's so much more to it. There's so much more to having a relationship with God. I had to realise this myself. I hope others do too.

So, here's my attempt to hurdle through the third thread of my mind, in hope that, it helps me. In hope that, it helps you.

March 2013

The time was nearing for exams, and I felt as though, I wasn't prepared at all. I was revising, but perhaps not as much? Truth be told, the last few months had been the longest months I'd experienced, and it's a miracle I'm standing here right now, staring down at these papers and hoping to make sense of it all. I was beginning to feel bit overwhelmed by it all, so I took out my little book and thought I'd write it down:

"Exams. Soon. Revision. Hardly." These were the only four words I was able to write,

Truth be told, writing helped me to make sense of things my mind would often find hard to comprehend. So I would write it all down, in the form of phrases, or statements or even long essays - just to unburden my mind of the constant thinking it was so adamant on doing. It began soon after I began to turn to Allah. I realised that if I wanted Him to help me, I also had to help myself. And in a way, writing would help. It would help me to come to terms with what I'm feeling. It would allow me to acknowledge the fact that if I'm capable of writing down these feelings, these thoughts, then I'm also capable of overcoming them. My first few pieces were full of darkness. They were empty. No hope. At all. But, it helped, you know? Here's one of the first things I wrote:

> "And the worst feeling is the feeling of numbness. Wanting to cry, but feeling as though your tears have dried up. Wanting to scream

but not finding the courage to speak. Almost as though you're entrapped in a cafe of broken feelings and shattered thoughts; your mind's weeping for help but your body is deaf to its cries."

Reading back on it now, when I'm not feeling as bad as I was in that moment, it feels dark. As though, I'm shocked that I can even experience that level of darkness. But, it's possible. And it happens, and if I were to sit here and contemplate how much this darkness is taking me away from my true self; then I wouldn't find myself automatically chasing the light. I wouldn't be happy straight away. It happens. It happens, and it'll happen.. I just need to accept it. I guess that's the first step right?

"DUNYA!!!!" Hawa screamed, literally snapping her fingers in front of my face.

"Damn.. what did I miss?" I said, looking as startled as ever.

She sat down next to me. And looked at me in the eyes.

"Hold up, what did you do now?"

It always starts with her trying to make some form of eye contact before she admits to doing something stupid. Or something I told her not to do.

"It's not me." She said, tears grasping at her eyes.

"Hawa.. you're worrying me now." I said, as my heart began to sink a little.

"But that's what you're doing to me." A tear falling escaping her eyes.

"What do you mean?" I asked.

25

In this moment, I was hoping, wishing, she wouldn't bring this up right now.

"I've tried so hard not to mention it, but I just want you to know you're not alone. And you don't have to do this to yourself."

"Stop Hawa." I said. The feeling of panic began to arise within my chest, and I was trying my best not to make it apparent.

"Okay." She said, clearly noticing how I was beginning to become uncomfortable.

I had to go. I had to go. I had to leave. I had to leave this situation.

"I need a moment." I said, trying with all the power I had, not to burst into tears.

I didn't leave.

I just sat there, trying my best to hold it within me. Praying to God that He would grant me that strength I always ask for, in this very moment. praying, that I wouldn't break down. I couldn't.
A few minutes passed. I looked up. I didn't have a panic attack. I was okay. I was actually o k a y.

"It's okay Hawa." I finally spoke.

She looked up, startled.

"I know that I probably haven't been the easiest to talk to the last few weeks, or even months. But it's okay. I'm coping. I don't know what else there is to say.."

"You don't need t.."

"No please, let me. I've just about gathered the courage to do this. So let me talk." I looked up, slightly making eye contact in the process.

"Okay, I'm listening." She said, reaching out to hold my hand.

"It's just. I'm not okay Hawa. I haven't been for a long time. I mean, I try so hard to make sure that I'm okay, that sometimes I even convince myself that I am. But, it's always there. It's following me. It's almost become my shadow; but one that stays with me for as long as I'm awake."

Hawa looked at me. I could see tears in her eyes. I didn't want to do this. I couldn't. I stopped.

"It's okay Hawa. I'm sorry... please don't cry. I won't talk about it."

"NO!" She immediately shot back. "This is NOT about me Dunya. This is about you. So for once, please, just let me be there for you.."

"Okay." I sighed.

It felt weird saying it all aloud. It felt surreal. How was I even feeling this way? How am I even capable of feeling this? I mean there's nothing wrong with my life (Alhamdhulillah). So how can I feel like this? Saying it out loud made me feel ungrateful.

"I've been.." I paused again. I can't do this.

"I've been har.."

"Harming yourself?" Hawa said. She didn't even seem surprised. I could just tell though. Her grip loosened, and her eyes dropped. She was disappointed in me.

"I know that Dunya."
"I saw your scars. I didn't want to say anything, because I am in no position to judge. But, I've been driving myself mad trying to get you to talk to me instead of resorting to that.."

"No Hawa. Please don't blame yourself. I've stopped. Well.. I'm trying. I've not done so in a while."

I could feel my eyes becoming heavy, and my tears soon failed to stay in. I let them flow.

"I've been praying more. I've been turning to Allah. I've used Him as my rock. He keeps me strong."

Hawa sighed. She held my hand again.

"I know. I know that sometimes all we need is a talk with our Creator to understand that we are not alone in this battle. I know this, because my mum has been through the same. I've seen this before. And I still do to this day. I know that she would rather talk to Her Lord, than talk to me. But that's okay. It's okay that sometimes you feel like that, because you understand that Allah is the only One worth trusting with everything you have. But sometimes, Allah tests us this way so that we can come to understand - that we don't just have Him, we have the people He has placed in our lives. You think our meeting was anything short of destiny? He knows that you and I needed each other. He knew that I needed you. He also knew that you needed me. Although, you're so strong,. You've been struggling all on your own.. He's sent me here, He's given you this courage to tell me everything, because He wants you to know: you are really not alone. No matter how much you may feel it.. you are not alone." She said, trying to comfort me.

At this point, I grabbed Hawa into a hug and just cried for a good minute.

She understood me. And for the first time in a while, I felt like, I was actually understood.

"Thank you Ha-"

"Don't you dare thank me." She said, pointing towards my nose and giving me a tissue in the process.

I let out a little smirk.

"You know Dunya, there's this one verse in the Qur'an. It says:

يَٰٓأَيُّهَا الَّذِينَ ءَامَنُوا اسْتَعِينُوا بِالصَّبْرِ وَالصَّلَوٰةِ ۚ إِنَّ اللَّهَ مَعَ الصَّٰبِرِينَ

'Seek help in patience and in Prayer; Allah is with those that are patient.' (Quran: 2:53)

When you hear those words, what's the first thoughts that come to mind?" She said, looking at me.

"Can I be honest? Although, at times I've been distant from Allah, every single time, I open the Qur'an and I read the words of Allah, I somehow feel as though there's parts of me becoming enlightened, you know? And this quote in particular, is just one of the many quotes from Allah, that has hope seeping through. Hope. It gives me so much hope. It's as though, all of a sudden? I feel powerful."

"Wow." Hawa said.

"I get you, because I feel the same. If I'm being completely honest, I've always been one to share the verses of the Qur'an without thinking so much about what they mean. But each word. Each and every word mentioned in the Qur'an, it's as though they were written, they were revealed to heal us.."

"You're right.." I said smiling.
"Allah is the Ultimate Healer. And I'm learning that now more than ever."

We continued to talk more about our goals, and how to stay on track with our deen, and promised each other to keep going. And overall? The day just felt so wholesome.

I stayed up a little longer that night. I didn't feel negative, but I didn't feel entirely content. It was somewhere in the middle. Strange. A part of me felt pain, and wanted to scream, and cry, like I had been doing the previous nights. And the other part of me, felt motivated. Felt enlightened. So I got out my notebook, and I wrote:

> "So often, when we're sent trials we become so consumed within the pain that comes with it, that we become lost in our pain. We become lost in trying to maintain our mental well-being and trying to fix things that have brought us to that very pinpoint in life. We almost forget that everything is pre-determined. That the pain we're feeling right now; it was written thousands of years before we were born. Of course, this doesn't mean that you should stop fighting, but whilst fighting don't forget to look in the right place. Know that it's all just a pathway. A pathway to seeking Allah. A pathway that'll also lead us to our future selves. Think of it like this. The trials you've been through in the past, the things you've gone through so

far; if you hadn't, would you be who you are in this moment of time? Would you have gained those skills it granted you? Would you have gained those crucial life lessons it's taught you? You see it's planned. Just like the pain you're feeling right now. It's all planned. And it's going to be okay. Because this pain wasn't sent to torture you. It wasn't sent to destroy you. It was sent to strengthen you. It was sent by the One who loves you more than your own loved ones do. It was sent so that you may seek that which has always sought you: Allah. And the closer you grow to Allah, the more you'll know - every single thing was meant to send you to that prayer mat, with your head placed on the ground and your heart echoing Allah's name. It was always meant to be this way. Always."

It felt good writing that out. In a way, although it was me writing it, its as though it was my soul reminding me that there is hope. That hope is here, with me, in me, in all things that surround me. All I had to do was let the hope carry me along. And so that's what I choose to do from now on.

I opened up my Qur'an again. This time, my heart seemed to be stuck on this verse:

وَلَا تَهِنُوا وَلَا تَحْزَنُو

Do not lose hope, nor be sad. [Qur'an 3:139]

As usual, I kept reading over it. As though, by reading these words, I would somehow engrave them into this stubborn heart of mine. I knew that I had to keep going. That all this motivation to pray, to read the Qur'an was really a blessing in disguise from Allah and I couldn't ignore it. So I had to keep going. I had to, because He believed in me enough to send me these blessings, I just had to believe in myself too.

4

That morning had come earlier than I even wanted it to. Which was odd, for me.

"Strange.." I muttered to myself.

It was 8AM and no missed calls from Hawa? By now she would have rang me a few times at least, to make sure I'm not late.

I decided to get ready and ring her on the way to college. I rang her once, but it went to voicemail. Even more strange.

I rang again.

"Hello" Hawa said, in the most dullest way possible.

"Okay, what's happened?" I immediately knew it. She wasn't herself, and she's rarely not herself.

"Um."

"You didn't?" I knew straight away what she might have done.

"Please say you didn't?"

"You can't be mad." She said, knowing full well that I was mad.

At this point I was almost running to college, so that I could see her face and ask her WHY.

"WHY?" I said, shouting down the phone and running up to her. She was sat in the middle of the corridor, tears streaming down her face, and struggling to even look up at me.

"Hawaaaa." I said, bringing her in for a hug.

"He is not worth it."

I knew it. She gave him another chance, and he broke her heart. Again. How is that even possible? It could be that I'm saying this because I've never experienced that heartbreak, but how can someone break your heart more than once and still you claim to love them? I don't know what love is. And truth is, I felt as though I didn't even want to know. Not if it meant that it would cause this level of heartbreak.

"I didn't know it would be like this again, I swear." She said, wiping her tears with her sleeve and gathering up the courage to talk.

"I told you Hawa. He's not good for you. All he's done is cause you harm-"

"Come on Dunya, you know that's not right. At the start he was so charming, so sweet. He cared about me so much. Even you thought that."

"Okay, but that was at the start Hawa. Look at what he's doing to you now. And tell me that this is love?"

"I don't know what it is. But it's hurting. It wouldn't hurt this much if it wasn't love."

"Maybe it is love on your behalf. But you can't know if it's the same for him. You can't know someone's intentions. I guess that's why it's a risk. I guess that's why some people say that falling in love is a risk. You fall in love, knowing full well what your intentions are, but you never know what their intentions are. You've spent so long creating this image of them in your heart, that you fall in love with that image. So when the inevitable happens, and they hurt you, you can't see it any other way. It's almost like your mind, your thoughts, everything that's happened, are going to war with your heart. Your mind is aware that they've done this, that they've hurt you, but your heart refuses to believe it. It refuses to view that person in any other light, than the positive one it's been looking through for so long. But regardless, that's not on you. The fault is in the love they claimed to have. How can he claim to love you and yet be the reason behind your tears? This is not love Hawa."

She nodded. She knew I was speaking sense. But right now, although it seemed like the best thing to say on my behalf, it's not what she needed to hear.

"It's okay. You're going to be okay. All is not lost. You have me."

She smiled a little.
We sat in silence for a few moments before the usual morning rush began and the college day had started.

She was quiet for the remainder of that day, as expected. You would be after a heartbreak right?

We sat in our usual spot after school and revised together. She was really focused. And then she looked up at me. I knew she wanted to say something, but she was withholding her words.

"What's up?" I said.

"Hmm." She said, looking down at her papers and then up at me again.

35

"How do you know?" She asked curiously.

"How do I know what?" I replied, eager to know what she wanted to ask.

"Like, how do you know about heartbreak if you haven't experienced love?"

"You know, you don't always have to experience something to know what it's like. Sometimes, things are felt even though it doesn't directly effect you." I spoke, looking at the wall in front of me and trying not to go off on a tangent.

"How though?" She said, intrigued as ever.

"I don't know. I guess, looking at you, and seeing what you've been through. It's taught me a lot. You know how everyone says that sometimes you have to experience certain things to learn valuable lessons? I feel like that applies in this situation, only I didn't directly experience it. It was you that experienced it, and yet it was me that felt it."

"You feel a lot. Maybe that's why it hurts so much." She said, seriousness filling the air.

"I guess you can say that. sometimes, I feel too much. And other times, I feel nothing at all. But if I'm honest, I'd rather feel it all at once."

"Why? Doesn't that hurt?"

"It does. But nothing hurts more than the feeling of numbness."

"I'm sorry." Hawa said. Eyes unable to face me and almost sounding like she was about to tear up.

"Come on now Hawa. I've told you not to apologise. I am the way I am, because of me. Because this is my mind, and this is my battle. What I feel, and what I think, is not your fault. It's not anyone's fault."

At this moment in time, I was regretting my speech. It reminded me of that quote: *"I've never regretted my silence. As for my speech? I've regretted it time and time again."*. It was kind of like that. Don't get me wrong, I was grateful for Hawa, But at the same time, I was beginning to feel like a burden on her. I felt like now that my mind had tackled its lonely thoughts, it was now beginning to turn to other things. Negative things, where I ask myself why I am here or why I am such a burden on people. I didn't know how to make this cycle stop. I mean, is it just continuous? Do I have to fight something off, and then get ready to fight a whole other battle again? Why must it be like this?

There was an awkward silence that followed that. We were both silent; but that silence spoke so loud. I knew I had to snap out of my thoughts, so that I can continue helping Hawa, so I tried my best to divert the attention to her again.

"So, did any of that make sense?"

"Most of it." She said, looking up at me and almost half smiling.

"You know Hawa.. before you met him, you were happy on your own terms. You refused to allow anyone to spoil that. You were very stubborn as to who you let in and who you don't."

"I know." She said.

"I know that Dunya, and a part of me feels regret more than anything. It feels like I've almost sabotaged my personality, my happiness, just for a temporary person.."

"That's the thing, I guess.. No-one is promised to us. When we meet certain people, they break down barriers we didn't think anyone could. And when they are successful in breaking down these barriers, we become impressed with them. We feel like, they were God-sent because of how smooth their entrance into our lives was.." This conversation was getting deep. There was something about deep conversations that drew me in. That enticed my soul and allowed it to feel at home. It felt like a second nature to me.

"But.. aren't all people God-sent Dunya? Take me and you as an example." Hawa said. At this point she was scrolling through her gallery and deleting photos, but she paused. And she looked up at me, awaiting an answer, an answer that will actually sit with her.

"Yeah. You're right. Every single person that comes into our lives, is there because Allah sent them there. Not everyone you meet in life will stay, for as long as you want them to. You see, everyone's on a journey, to Allah. And along that journey, you've gotta meet several people. Some that will walk with you until you reach the next milestone. Some that will help you, until they leave you to find your own path, and so that they can find theirs too. And some that will walk with you through to the very end. But each one of these people are there to shape you into the person you were always meant to become. Which is why, I've never believed in meeting people by accident; it's always for a reason. And even if the reason hurts, we learn from the hurt too, right?" I paused, awaiting her response.

"Right." Hawa said, so intrigued with what I was saying.

"Please carry on.. it's actually sinking in. You make so much sense with your words Dunya.."

"So, I guess, what I'm trying to say is that don't worry if you're not the same happy person on your own terms again. It's okay. Because you are forever growing, forever changing; you will meet several people, and they will all have different affects on you. Hence, you will never be the same person. We can stop people from coming into our lives, but if they're destined to be there, then we can't compete against God's will. So perhaps, his entrance into your life, although short lived, was meant to happen. It was meant to happen, so that you can understand your value. It hurts now, but the more you turn to Allah, the more you'll come to understand that everything He did was for your benefit. So, take this as a sign. That Allah knew you were becoming lost in someone other than Him, so He called you back. So that you may experience real love.. real peace.. real happiness."

"Wow." Hawa said, sounding almost startled at what I said.

"Thank you. Thank you so much. Can I be honest?" She asked.

I nodded and waited for her to speak.

"Right now, I'm feeling a lot of pain. A lot of heartbreak. And your words have helped. Trust me, when I say they have. But I guess, it'll take time for it to actually sink in, right?"

"Of course Hawa. No-one expects you to heal from this quickly. There's no time limit on how long you should take to heal from this. Sometimes, we become so hasty in wanting a part of our lives to come to an end, that we don't acknowledge that we need to live in the moment, if it means we truly want to move forward.."

At this point, I took her hand and said: "Take as long as you need. Just remember you are not alone. I'm here. And above all, Allah is here. With you, always."

I was a little worried for Hawa. But, being a friend, who wouldn't be? Don't get me wrong, I know she was capable of overcoming this trial that was sent to her. But at the same time, I was scared of how she would bear the heartbreak, again. Although.. the first heartbreak was harder on her than this. I mean, this time, it felt different. It felt like, she knew what she had to do. And she had enough. Almost as though, she knew that she had to stop living in this bubble she created for herself, so she wanted to snap out of it. But as much as she wanted to do that, is her heart going to side with her mind? Is she going to listen to her mind, is she going to convince her heart that she doesn't need him as much as she needs herself? I hope so. I really do.

5

I woke up the next morning, thinking about Hawa. I wondered how she was holding up. I began thinking about what Hawa asked me. How do I know what heartbreak is if I've never been in love? Love? What is love to me?

I began to write.

> I've always believed, from what I've seen, from what I've experienced, that love is not meant to make you feel weak. At least, true love.. Love is defined as something that moves two hearts; not just one. Saying this, of course it isn't just confined to romantic relationships, but family and friends too. Love is more than the heartbreak you feel when you become distant from someone you were once attached to. Love is more than the sadness you feel when you see someone you liked, with someone else. Love is in the way your mother struggled to strive when everything was pulling her back, yet she lived on for you. Love is in the way your father worked long hours and hardly saw you, just to put food on the table. Love is when Allah forgave you. When He took you from where you once were; lost, wandering, no destination in sight, and gave you meaning. Love is when you searched for companionship and found it in the form of friendships you hold dear to your heart. Love is with you, around you, happening in every moment you breathe.

"Okay." I sighed, reading back over it.
It felt a bit heavy reading over it and still not being able to understand just how much Hawa was hurting. I stopped my thoughts from spiralling out of control and decided to ring her.

It rang twice and she answered.

"Hm morning." She said, half asleep.

"Wow! You're still asleep? I mean YOU, I mean HAWA is still asleep?"

"HAHA, so funny Dunya."

"No but seriously, it's almost 8AM and you're normally at college by now?" I said in a slightly concerned tone.

"I don't think I'm coming in today. I've had a long night, and I kinda just want to sleep in." Hawa said, almost sounding like she was about to tear up.

"No Hawa, I won't let you do this. You NEED to come. You've been like this the entire weekend, and I admit, there's nowhere to even go during the weekend, but now you have somewhere to go. And the more you stay in bed, the worse you'll feel. You want to feel better don't you?"

"Hm yeah." She muttered.

"Hawa, if you don't get up and get ready, I will personally come there and force you."

I felt a bit bad, but at the same time, I know that this is what she needed. I know that when I was at my worst, I wanted to stay in bed all day, every day. But at the same time, I wanted to have a motive. I wanted to fix how I feel and just distract myself with things that mattered. I wanted her to see that life still goes on.

"Okay okay, keep your hijab on will you?" She said, yawning in the process. I could hear her moving about in the background. Sounded like she was actually going to listen to me.

"Okay, I'll see you in college at half 8?"

"K."

"Did.. you… just?"

"It's a date." She quickly said as she cut the call.

I let out a little scoff and laughed. I knew she was trying her best to feel better by lightening the mood, and plastering a smile over her hurting heart. I wanted her to feel okay, but I also hoped that she didn't completely silence her emotions and all that she felt. I guess, that's something I've learnt myself. I've learnt that, even though I want to feel better, I can't rush the process. I can't completely block everything out and paint over it all, expecting to be magically okay. Because it won't. There has to be some sort of balance, you know? Like I need to try. And I need to try with all the fight I have left in me, but I also need to let myself feel, I need to acknowledge that those feelings, those emotions are there. And they are there for a reason.. so that I can feel them. So that I can come to terms with them.

There I was.. going off on a thinking trail again.

I got ready and went down to have breakfast as usual. My mum was awake, which wasn't weird, as she would normally be up and making breakfast for everyone, ensuring everyone's ate before they've started their days.

"What time will you be back today?" She said, looking over at my shambles of a breakfast, and passing me a plate with toast on it instead.

"Normal time." I said, smiling at her thoughtful gesture.

"Okay."

I noticed her looking at me a few times. I didn't say anything. I had this feeling that she wanted to ask me something, but she was holding back. So I asked instead.

"Did you need to ask me something?"

She paused for a second. She looked down and then up at me again, locking her eyes in mine.

"Are you okay?"

"Yeah, why wouldn't I be?" I lied.

"It's just you never spend time with us anymore. You're always in your room. And when you're not there, you're at college.."

She was beginning to notice. Notice that I wasn't myself. I was different. I could feel panic arising within my chest, but at the same time, I knew that if I couldn't tell my mum, then who would I tell?

"No, it's nothing. Just college stress." I lied.
It slipped? I guess although I knew that she was my mum, and that she would probably understand, at the same time, I didn't know how to say anything? So I just didn't.

"Okay. Try not to stress. Just keep studying and focus on your studies, and ask your teachers if you need any extra support." She said.

My mum wasn't educated in the UK, nor in Pakistan, where she was born and lived most her childhood. I guess, it was normal during her time, to get married young and just make a life for yourself. She's told me several stories about her. And how different life was for her, than it is for me and my sibling. How she would be expected to do all the house chores at a young age, but it was normal, so she wouldn't complain.. like me and my sibling do sometimes. I mean who doesn't, right? She would never say that we have it easy, but we should motivate us to do better. To take full advantage of the things we have, that she didn't.

I guess, I was close to my mum. But at the same time, I wasn't. I felt solace in her stories, in her words. I guess, that's why I felt like I never had it in me to tell her that I was feeling such a way. In a way, I was scared about her mental well-being, more than mine. I know that she would probably overthink it, and blame herself. And ask herself what she might have done. But mental health is not like that. And not many people understand that. I mean, living in the community that we do, mental health is always blamed on something. Almost like: "you're feeling suicidal? But why? What happened? Did I do something? Do so and so do something? You're feeling anxious? But why? You're feeling unhappy? Why, you've got so many good things going for you? Are you ungrateful?"

It's a never-ending cycle of toxicity. Another reason for why I feel like, whatever I feel? I must keep to myself. Because no-one will understand the way I understand it. To them, it might just be that I'm ungrateful, or that I'm attention seeking, but to me it's nothing like that. It never has been. And at times, I wish, that it was just that. It would probably be easier to explain.

"Okay Mum. I'm off now. Khuda-Hafiz." I said, looking back at her once, and noticing that she looked tired. Was it because of me? Was I being selfish for not telling her how I feel? I felt guilty, but at the same time I felt as though it would make her feel worse.

I thought about her all throughout my walk to college. I had my earphones on, but no music playing. I was just lost in my thoughts, as usual.

As I got into college, I hoped that Hawa was there. And there she was. Sat at the table, her books in front of her, reading her work. She was squinting, which is what she does when she doesn't understand something. It was funny watching her do that. She knew I would always tease her for it.

"BOO!" I sneaked up from behind her. She did not move. Not a single bit.

"Wow, you scared me Dunya! It's not like I saw you coming in from the window right next to me."

"Sarcasm does not suit you, especially when you're squinting like that." I laughed, hoping to get some kind of positive reaction out of her.
She smiled and rolled her eyes.

"So what you working on?"

"My notes.. you know.. for the exam we have this week?"

"Yeah, about that.."

"You haven't started?" She gasped, in the most sarcastic way possible.

"HAHA, hilarious! Now let's revise."

We didn't have much lessons that day, so we spent most of it revising whatever we could, and stopping each other from being stress-heads. I tried not to talk about my mental health, and although I noticed Hawa lost in her thoughts a couple times, I also tried not to ask her about how she was. I kept reminding her to focus and gave that reassuring look, as to say, that it will be okay. We just need to get through this bit, and then we can focus more so on what we need to do to heal.

The next few days were heavy. I felt stress and panic, and was surviving on hardly any sleep. I mean, it's not like I would be able to get that much sleep anyways. But, revising constantly meant that I had to make sure I slept late and woke up as early as possible. But by the end of the exam period, you'd expect it to feel better. Like you can finally breathe. I didn't.

The last day of college was upon us, and I couldn't help but think about what I would do distract myself now? It's like, during the days I would have all this, revision, college, and Hawa to keep me distracted. But now, I was almost scared? Scared about my mental health, but also about how I would possibly react to everything going on in my mind. It's like now, I had all this time, with nothing in particular to keep me from thinking.

I was sat with Hawa and a few other friends in the canteen. They were talking and laughing as usual. I smiled a few times, as to try and convince them that I'm with them on this. But it felt like I was there, but I wasn't. I could feel my chest tightening, and the sense of panic taking over. I had to remove myself from here, before it starts.

"Erm, I'll be back. Just going to the bathroom." I said, not allowing anyone to reply and leaving in a rush.

I shot past everyone and got to an empty cubicle. I sighed. I covered my mouth. And I tried to cry. I couldn't cry. There were no tears. But why I was I finding it so hard to breathe? Why was I feeling this panic, without actually feeling the need to cry? Nothing made sense.

There was a knock on my door.

"Dunya?" It was Hawa.

"Dunya, come out, please?"

Did I make it too obvious? I felt a tear roll down my cheeks. They had begun. The tears had begun. I checked the time, it was 1:30PM. Zahur had begun. I just knew, that in this instance, I wanted to be in front of Allah. I wanted to be talking to Him. I took a few deep breathes, and gathered a little courage to be able to reply to Hawa.

"Yeah, just doing my Wudu."

"Okay.." She said, not sounding convinced at all.

"I'll do mine too."

I did my Wudu, and left the cubicle.

"Shall we pray?"

She led the way to the prayer room, and thankfully, there was no-one there. I assumed that most students had left and gone home, or out to celebrate. I immediately began to read and I could just feel my tears rolling down my cheeks. Almost like, Allah was telling me that this tears need to be shed so that I can cleanse my mind. So that I can cleanse my thoughts. So that I can feel okay. It was okay to cry, especially in front of the One that knew why I was crying, even if I didn't. As usual, I didn't want to leave the prayer mat, so I sat there and looked at my hands. I held them up high and I let my tears talk for me.

"Ya Rab. Ya Rab."

These were the only words that had the courage to escape my lips. I did not know what else to say. But, at the same time I knew that words did not have to be uttered for feelings to be understood. For my thoughts to be understood. He knew what I was feeling. I just had to sit there. I just had to cry. So that perhaps, I can come to understand, why I was feeling. So that perhaps, I can feel some strength. I finished my due and lowered my hands, and looked to Hawa. She was sat with her eyes closed and her hands raised. I could tell she was feeling that same heartbreak. I almost felt like she was afraid of the same things I was afraid of too. But the reminder of that day, we were quiet. It's like we had a lot to say, but we couldn't find the words. So we decided to remain quiet.

I hugged her a little longer that day, knowing that it was the last time we'd see each other for a while. Not until results day.. but let's not talk about that right now? We promised to make our meetings weekly when university started, but we both kind of knew that was unrealistic.

6

The summer was upon us. The much dreaded summer.
I wasn't really a summer person. I think it had more to do with the fact that I would not have anything to keep me busy, rather than the actual heat.. but then again, you can never rely on British weather, so the heat was also kind of a let down.

I walked home that day, and listened to my favourite nasheed on repeat. In she Allah by Maher Zain. It often brought me to tears and reminded me that Allah is with me, always. That no matter how far I was from the prayer mat, He was there. He is with me always. Watching over me always.

When I got home that day, I saw my mother standing before me, looking down and crying. I instantly felt my heart sinking. I knew something had happened..

"Your Nani.."

Wait, what?

"Your nani has left this world."

I instantly broke into tears.

I hugged my siblings a little longer that day, as we all shared the pain and tried to be there for our mum, who had just lost her mother. The next few days were a blur. Every time someone comforted me, it felt as though they were just uttering empty words. As though they were speaking, but nothing was sitting right with me. Nothing was convincing me that it'll be okay. So I knew, the One that could comfort me, is Him and so I turned to Him more.

"Ya Allah.
I ask of you to bring my mum's heart peace. Let her feel okay. Let her feel
at peace. Protect her."

At times, I felt stupid asking this. Because I knew that it was hurting, and it was bound to hurt her for as long as she lived. Losing a mother isn't something that leaves you so soon. The feelings are going to be there. As long as she breathes.

At the same time, I asked myself several questions. Is this what heartbreak feels like? A lot of people talk about heartbreak, and when they do, they connect it to romantic relationships. But, heartbreak is not limited to just that, right?

"I guess, this dunya and all that contains is there to cause heartbreak."
I began to write.
"I guess, it was always meant to be this way. It's like, ever since the moment we are born. We are attached to our parents, or our carers. We become uneasy when they are not around, and they do too. We grow and we become attached to several other things. To people. To things. To things that can be taken away, as easily as we gained them. We become attached to ideas. To beliefs. To goals. But, when they're taken away, what are we left with? Emptiness. Emptiness that remains with us, because we've spent so long, so long, giving away pieces of ourselves to things and people that we have encountered. I guess that's the whole point though, right? I mean, it's normally when we're at our lowest we tend to search for answers. For support. And most times, we find ourselves on the prayer mat, sat in front of the Only One capable of giving those answers. The Only One capable of being there. The only One that

doesn't break our hearts, yet is the reason for why our hearts are mended so often. I guess, every person that's taken away, whether it be a parent, grandparent, or even romantic partner, is taken away for a reason. Perhaps, their time in our lives had come to an end. Perhaps their time on this world had come to an end. Perhaps, it was time, that we stood back from our hasty lives and reevaluated the real reason as to why we are here. For why Allah has placed us here. Perhaps, it's time to let us realise that even though, right now, they are not with us, if we work hard enough for our hereafter, like we do so for our life on this planet, we will reunite in Jannah. Maybe, it's Allah giving us chance after chance, to prove that we are worthy of Jannah. But at the same time, He's reminding us that our hearts will always break. It's the dunya. It was always a place for testing."

I'll be honest. At times, I would begin writing, and it would seem as though it made sense. But then, it was as though it was going with the flow. My heart would flow into words that I didn't think I had within me, and often, I'd find myself going off on a tangent. But no matter how abnormal that tangent was, it always somehow made sense to me. So I would read it, read it again and again, almost as a way of me reassuring myself that if I could write it, there must be some strength within me to be able to get through whatever it is that made me want to write it down.

I spent the next few weeks, trying to figure some things out. I didn't know where all this curiosity was coming from. Or perhaps I was just in search of answers for questions that had been buried for too long, and were brought to the surface with the pain I felt. I asked myself, what is the difference between a temporary one and an eternal one? I asked myself, what is love? Why is love glamourised if it's just meant to bring pain? What is it's purpose?

I wrote a lot. A lot more than expected.

"Love. If you had asked me, a few years ago, what is love? I would have responded by saying "love is not real". I would have responded by telling you that love doesn't live in reality. It lives within movies, where unrealistic expectations are placed. But now, I know more than that. Like I've said before, love is bound to more than just romantic relationships. But there's a difference between a love that doesn't hurt and a love that does. At times, we think that love is not meant to hurt. But anything or anyone that we come to love on this Earth will always hurt. The only love that won't hurt, is the love that lives forever, within us, and that's the love for Allah. I guess, that's the difference between a humanly love and a Godly one - it doesn't hurt. I guess, that's the whole point of this life right? Like if this life was easy, if love was easy, we wouldn't want it. The whole point of life being a test is that we want the life. But to overcome it, we must come to understand that what we want and what we need, are two very different things. We think we want love, a love that doesn't hurt, but what we need is Allah's love and we can only acquire that once we do what we can to please Him. We think we want all this dunya has to give, when in reality we need the afterlife. It doesn't need us, yet we need it. It's almost as though, throughout it all, our souls are speaking to us. They are telling us to take certain directions, because they know those directions are best for us. They are best for our heart. And all in all, we always end up in one place: in front of Him. So, you see, we think we want human love, but Allah's love is the only love we need. I've come to learn, just how freeing that is.. you know? To understand Allah's love for us. It's like, falling backwards into a river but knowing nothing will harm you because Allah is there to help you float at the surface. It's like, taking a test, but not worrying so much about the result because you know, that whatever the result is, has some goodness written in it for you. I guess, a part of understanding Allah's love for us is knowing that Allah's plans are better. That even if His plans don't make sense in the moment, they will in the long term. Because He loves us. So He wants best for us, more than we want best for ourselves."

I sighed.

It was like, after every time I wrote, I felt a burden leaving my chest. As though, previous to this I was finding it hard to breathe. I was grasping for air, but there was not enough air present around me, for me to actually breathe. It was suffocating, to put it simply.

I made it a habit to open up the Qur'an every time I couldn't make sense of my own words, because I knew His words were the words that actually mattered.

وَّتَوَكَّلْ عَلَى اللّٰهِ ۗ وَكَفٰى بِاللّٰهِ وَكِيْلًا

Put your trust in Allah: Allah is sufficient as Guardian. [Qur'an 33:3]

Reading these words, it was as though Allah was telling me that I wouldn't be disappointed with having Tawwakul: full faith in His plan for me. I knew that I had to continue this journey to healing with full confidence in Allah. Allah is enough for me. Allah's guidance is enough for me to get through this.

7

The next few weeks seemed to go slower than I wanted them to. I wanted to be past this point in life. I wanted to leave this point in my life, and somehow escape to a few years ahead. Perhaps, then, I would know if it does actually get better, like everyone promises that it does.

I guess, the good thing to come from this year was that I passed my A-Levels and got into university. The university I wanted to go. I had a chance to start again. But new beginnings, were never easy. Especially for me. It took a while for me to try and become used to something new. And university was one of those. So, expectedly, I found it hard. Really hard. I didn't know anyone. I hated being the first to create conversation, as it always felt too fake and forced. I never knew how to do that, without feeling as though I wanted to crawl down a hole and evaporate from the face of the Earth. Is that possible? (If so, do let me know how).

"Morning everyone! And welcome to your first day at university. I can see that you've all been handed your timetables and a welcome pack to go with it. Your lectures will commence from next week, but this week will be an introduction into what you can expect from university in the coming years."

"He seems nice." A voice spoke from next to me.

I looked up, and it was another hijabi. All of a sudden, I felt at ease.

"Haha, he does. Let's hope he lives up to that."

"I'm Saha, wbu?"

"Dunya, it's nice to meet you."

"So what are you studying?"

"Theology with Education Studies, and you?"

"Ah, I guess we'll be seeing each other a lot then. I'm also taking Education Studies, but with English."

For one, I hated small talk, but I knew I had to start somewhere. I couldn't spend the entire three years at university isolating myself from others right?

"That's good to know! What made you choose this university then?"

"Totally wanted to move out, but knew with Asian parents, that would be impossible, so came to the one with the furthest commute." We both laughed.
It was kind of true though. I mean, I didn't choose this university for that reason, but I enjoyed long commutes.

"I guess there's always a blessing with staying at home though. Least we won't have to cook for ourselves."

"True, true! Couldn't possibly live without my mum's cooking."

"Talking about food.. I'm staaarrrving. Shall we eat?" I said, looking at the food people were carrying past.

"Please! Let's."

I hung around with Saha for the rest of that day, and it's safe to say we kind of made friends? I didn't feel completely isolated and actually for once enjoyed somewhere where Hawa wasn't. I, of course told Hawa all about my day, and she was her overprotective best friend self.

"So.. I'm not distracting you from talking to your new bestie right now am i?"
I couldn't stop laughing. We always found a way to be goofy.
It was the best part of my day, coming home to ring Hawa and just talk about our days. At times, we wouldn't even talk and just have each other in the background. It was nice to know that I'd always have her, and that our friendship didn't just stop at the end of college.

––––––––––

A few weeks had passed by, and I was already feeling the stresses of uni. I mean, I must have considered dropping out a total of 7 times. Wait, that's a lie. It's way more than that. In fact, I think I might have lost count already. Despite this, I've always been intrigued by education studies and ethics, which is why I chose this degree in particular. I was attending all my lectures and trying my best to familiarise myself with how to become a top university student.

My mental health was okay at this point. I felt like I completely immersed myself in my education, so much so that I didn't allow myself to have that 'thinking' time. Although, at times, the thoughts would come to me whilst sat idle in a lecture, or on the way back from university, I would try to brush them off. In a way, it would help, but I kind of knew that the inevitable would happen, and I would break. I knew my mind too well by now.

My spiritual journey was still existent. I still tried my best to pray my prayers on time and connect to Allah. I knew I am nothing without Him, and I was trying to embed that knowledge into everything. I even joined the islamic society at university. It was very insightful, and I met some influential sisters.

I remember exactly how I felt in those first two months at university, and to put it simply, I felt surreal. It felt surreal. It felt like I was in an alternate universe where problems didn't exist unless I allowed them to exist. And I tried so hard to make sure they didn't, but I knew they were there. But, you know what they say about surrealism? It's a fantasy. A dream. And dreams only last for the moments you are asleep. They are short lived. And perhaps, that's exactly what this was.

I remember the date. It was the 22nd of November. It was the day everyone was going to receive their results for the first assignment we were given. I remember, letting this day determine how I would spend the rest of my time at university, and til this day? I don't have any regrets. None at all.

"So?" Saha said, peaking over at my computer.

"I passed, Alhamdhulillah." I said, grinning, and reading the feedback to myself.

"Oh.. you got 50? Don't worry, in sha Allah next time you'll do better.."

"Wait, what?"

"You got 50.. it's just about a pass.."

"I mean, for a first assignment and first attempt at writing something at degree level, I'd say that was good."

61

"I mean, good for you.."

"Wow."

I ignored anything else she said, and continued to read my feedback. But that wasn't the worse off it.

"Saha! Hey, how are you?"

Saha had her own group of friends. She was a lot more out going than I was, and pretty much talked to anyone. I wasn't like that.

I could hear whispering, so I looked up and saw them looking at me. This is so stupid, I thought to myself. As short lived as this friendship (if we're still calling that) was, it did hurt. I honestly felt so much less anxious knowing I had someone to share my university experience with, but the way that Saha and her group of friends were behaving, it made me think, do I even need someone to get me through this when I've gotten through the worst parts of my life all alone?

"No way." Lisa spoke, almost seeming like she was about to cry.

"I got 49.."

"Wait, let me check mine." Saha said, instantly going into shock mode as she opened her emails.

"This can't be real, right?"

"Dunya…"

"Save it Saha." I said, gathering my things and leaving.

I guess, this is the defining part of my entire university experience. It was kind of the reason why I became the way I did, and the reason for why I can't say, "I have university friends" because that would be a lie. To be honest, I felt it a lot the first few months. I would sit alone at lunch, and would always find myself booking a computer in the 'silent' part of the library. I guess in a way, it was good for me because I got all my work done without any distractions. But then, I started to go university less and less. I guess, a part of me didn't like the way it made me feel. I felt like an outsider looking in, but not wanting to be a part of the 'in'. I wanted to be alone, I was okay with being alone.. at least that's how I reassured myself.

I was at it again… away with my thoughts, whilst travelling to see Hawa. I hadn't seen her in a whole week and I felt like it had been months. I know, a week really is a long time! I was looking forward to it. She did say she had some important news, but knowing Hawa it would probably be something like 'I finally grew my broken nail back'.

I was stopped in my thinking tracks by a hand waving in my face. I looked up.

'Wow' I whispered to myself, thinking about how rude that gesture was.

"Yes?"

"Is anyone sat here? I wouldn't normally wave like that because I'm not rude or anything but I saw you had earphones in so kinda had no other option.."

"No, sorry, I'll move my bag."

I always had a habit of placing my bag in the seat next to me on public transport. Some might think it's selfish (which I kind of understand), but for me it was more of a 'don't sit next to me because I'm genuinely too awkward to ask you to move and I'll stay on the bus until you get off just so I don't have to talk.'

My stop was nearing, and you'd never guess what I was doing for the whole ten minutes this stranger was sat next to me? PRACTICING MY LINES. What? Don't laugh. ITS NORMAL. Okay maybe not. But anyways, the time had come to ask and he got up but just to give me way..

"Wait did I ask?"

"No, but I must have overheard you whisper it to yourself more so in the last 60 seconds, so I assumed this stop must be it.."

"Oh wow.. that is so embarrassing.."

"Now, please don't apologise again.."

I smiled and walked off the bus. He was odd. In a nice way?

I kept thinking about that as I was walking towards Hawa.. but I wasn't that lost in my thoughts that I didn't see her face gleaming with happiness. She sprinted towards me and hugged me.

"Not dramatic at all Hawa"

"Haha, shush, I'm just glad to see you."

"Okay, same.. but like… people…"

"OH DUNYA, will you just chill?"

I laughed and we carried on walking until we found a bench and Hawa was literally begging me to sit at this point.. and now I was worried. What could this news be?

"So?" I asked

"So, there's this.."

"GUY?"

"Wow you even finish my sentences for me.." Hawa was giggling. She was happy. I hadn't seen her genuinely happy for a while.

"But the thing is.. it's Amar.."

"WAIT WHAT?"

"I know.. I know. I'm aware of everything he's put me through. But he's serious now, and he's coming to ask for my rishta tomorrow Dunya. I'm so happy, I can't even express."

"Hawa.. you know whenever you're happy, I'll always be happy for you.. and I don't want to be negative but.."

"Okay then don't.. please.."

"Okay, I won't. But if he ever hurts you again, I swear-"

"Yeah I'll kill him with you don't worry." She laughed.

I was genuinely worried. This is the same guy that Hawa was dreaming of marrying in sixth form and it didn't work out. I remember just how heartbroken she was then. I remember the times she didn't look after herself for him. And the immense she felt. I remember it all. Because I was the only one to see her through it. I just didn't want the same to happen again.

You see, Amar was toxic, to say the least. He was the first guy she ever spoke to, but he was also the one that was there for her through one of the hardest parts of her life. And he kind of used that fact to get her, you know? He constantly reminded her of how much he did for her, and at first I thought Hawa was just grateful, but he had gotten into her head so much, that she eventually fell for him, as well as his tricks. She didn't like hearing a word against him, even when she knew he was in the wrong. And I really don't think this was love. I felt like it was more of her settling because she couldn't possibly imagine a life with another guy. But, she was worth so much more than settling.. she just didn't see it. I prayed for the day she would.

"So.." I said, breaking the silence, as she was eagerly going through her pictures and showing me what she had already thought about for her wedding.

"What you wearing tomorrow?" I asked, trying to hide the fact I was more concerned than happy. But I knew that I had to hold my silence for her. Maybe, it was one of those things she had to accept herself?

"So, I'm wearing the outfit that I wore on Eid. The silk kurta with trousers, and doing my makeup all nice.. but wait.."

'Yeah?"

"You are free tomorrow, right?" She asked, looking up at me all serious.

"My BEST friend is going to get engaged and I won't be free? PUH-LEASE." I said sarcastically, laughing mid-sentence.

"Anyways, can we shop now?" I said, forcing her up from the bench and putting her phone in my pocket.

"That's staying there for the next few hours because you're too into it."

"Okay Mum, that's fine." We both giggled away and began shopping. Once we started.. there was no stopping us.

I came home that day, and I felt inspired to write. I guess, thinking about Hawa and her situation influenced me to do so. So, I got out my book and I wrote…

"It's crazy isn't it? How Allah places certain people in our lives, and majority of the time? They're placed there to teach us lessons. Lessons that we wouldn't learn otherwise. And with these inevitable lessons, comes a lot of pain. Pain that we can't seem to fathom or put into words. Pain, that we feel only belongs to us. We let that pain, dictate the way we feel about everything.. just not including those people. We spend the majority of our time trying to heal from the pain. We learn what works for us, and what doesn't. And then they return. The same people that once taught us these lessons, return. They return in all their glory and come with several promises. They speak, and we believe what they say. Not because we completely trust them again, but because they've still got that hold over us. You know that pain we hold onto? Yeah, that's them having that hold over us. We assume that our prayers have been answered and they have finally arrived to fix what they broke.. our

67

hearts. But is it always like this? How can it be possible to trust someone again after them breaking your trust once? At times, I become unfaithful about love. I ask myself how love can possibly be so weak yet so strong at the same time? How can it be, that you love them so much that you're willing to forgive them, yet you're putting your heart at risk of being broken again. How is it possible? I guess, a part of me has always believed in the the kind of love that doesn't break, nor does it break you. But I guess for a lot of people, love is pain. I've heard a lot of people say, or even ask, how it can be love if it doesn't hurt? Maybe, in some ways they are right. But, love for me, is about happiness. And it'll stay that way. I hope I stick by this, no matter who enters my life."

I read over it several times and sighed. I felt as though there was something missing. As though, maybe I've not experienced that kind of love so I cannot possibly know what it feels like to be broken by it.

I remember praying a little more that night. I prayed for Hawa, and I prayed that she was putting her heart in a safe place. I know from past experience, Amar wasn't exactly a safe place, but I hoped what she said was true and he has changed. For her sake, more than anything.

8

"DUNYA YOUR ALARM WOKE ME UP, NOW WAKE UP!" I heard my brother literally screaming from outside my room.

"Wow. What a way to wake someone up!" I exclaimed back.

I looked at my phone and saw the time. It was 10:40 and I was still in bed! Maybe, all the thinking and writing last night took it out of me.

I scrolled down and saw FIFTEEN missed calls from Hawa. I rang her back instantly, wondering what it could be.

"DUNYA"

"YES?"

"WHERE ARE YOU?"

"Where normal people are at this time in the morning.. in bed." I said sluggishly.

"Yeah but they're coming in 4 hours!!!" She began to waffle about all she still has to do.

"Hawa.." No, didn't work, she carried on.

"Hawa.."

"HAWA" I shouted.

"YES?" She finally stopped.

"It's okay to be nervous. Just please don't go crazy, I'll be there in an hour."

"An.."

I cut off as soon as I said that, as I knew she'd be going even more crazy. I knew I had to go as soon as to calm her down.

I made my way to Hawa's with all the jewellery and makeup I had, and tried not to look at my phone whilst doing so, as I knew she'd be ringing me non-stop.
I finally got to hers and rang the doorbell.

"FINALLY" she opened it and dragged me in.

"Salam Aunty, you okay?" I asked her mum as she began pulling me up the stairs.

"No time for conversation Dunya!" Hawa exclaimed.
I couldn't help but laugh. But I also, kind of, felt nervous for her too. I really hope it works out.

Two hours later and Hawa was finally ready. What I mean by ready is that she was finally content with the outfit we had picked and hadn't taken it off to change for a whole ten minutes.

"Okay, it's this one."

"Awwwww, look at you glowing, you look so beautiful."

"Say Ma sha Allah." Her mum said walking in and smiling.

"Of course Aunty! Always!"

Hawa's phone began to rang so she went to answer it.

"So, what do you think?" Aunty said, with the same concerning look I had when Hawa told me about this.

"If she's happy, then I'm happy for her."

"I kind of feel like she ain't. I really don't like this guy." Aunty said, trying to hold her tears back.

"I know. But maybe we just need to see how this will pan out for Hawa's sake?"

Hawa came back into the room and began walking up and down constantly.

"Hawa?" I asked.

"They are nearly here." She said, taking a seat and looking scared.

"Okay, don't be nervous. It'll be okay." Her mum said as she got ready to go back downstairs.
Once she left, Hawa didn't say a word for a whole ten minutes.. which you should know by now.. is quite unusual.

"I feel like something's wrong." Hawa finally said.

"What do you mean?"

"I mean, he said he's coming but he didn't sound too happy."

"Aw, maybe he's stuck in traffic or maybe he just couldn't talk much in front of his family? I feel like you might be overthinking it because you're so nervous."

"You're right."

"See, that didn't take much convincing!" I said, throwing a pillow at her. We both laughed.

The evening had arrived, and Hawa was now engaged. I was so happy for her, but I just couldn't budge this feeling of anxiousness. I kept telling myself that I would feel better once she's married and he's actually proven that he's changed. But I also kept asking myself if I was a true friend for letting her go through with this. I mean, it's not as though Hawa would listen to me if I said 'don't' but it's the thought that counts, right? I just felt so conflicted and I didn't know what to do. But I know this must be harder on her Mum. I just feel like mothers have a good instinct about things. They know what's good for their children, and she knew, he wasn't it for Hawa. But we both promised to be quiet, just as long as she was happy. Because, believe you me, she was so happy.

The Nikkah was set for a date in six months time, so we had plenty of time to prepare. Hawa didn't want a big wedding, and luckily for her, neither did her fiancé. We spent majority of days planning and ensuring we have got everything right, because Hawa was adamant that she wanted it to be perfect.

But then came the third heartbreak..

It was 3AM in the morning and my phone was constantly vibrating. It was Hawa.
I answered.

"Hello?"

I could hear her crying down the phone.

"You were right." she said.

She was crying a lot so her words didn't seem as clear.
My heart sunk for her. At this point, I didn't want to be right.

"Hawa, I know nothing I say right now will seem like it makes sense, but please please try to stop crying so much, and just breathe. You know those breathing exercises you told me to do when I was crying over my Nan? Please do them Hawa. I just don't want you to begin panicking more than you are right now. Please."

"Ok." She said, as I talked her through it.

A few minutes later, and she had stopped crying.

"Okay, now please get some sleep, and I promise I'll be there first thing in the morning. I just think you've had a long night and I want you to be able to rest whilst you're calm and not thinking so much about it. I'll stay on the phone with you."

"Okay" she sighed and I could hear her fidgeting around in the background.

It was now 8AM, and her call was still on. I could hear her snoring (yeah she snored a lot). So I thought I'd get to hers before she woke up. I knocked on the door to her house, and her mum opened it.

"8:30AM? Where are you two off today?" Her mum said welcoming me in.

She seemed normal. I don't think she knows.

"Oh you know, our usual antics." I said, making my way to Hawa's room.

"Hawa?" I said, shaking her to wake up.

"Hmmm." She mumbled, half asleep.

"Come on, get up, we're going out."

"Its early, let me sleep." She mumbled again.

"Nope, get up!" I said lifting the duvet cover off her and opening the blinds.

"Okay okay, I'm up. But I'm coming in my night clothes."

"Fair enough, you're driving anyways."

"The cheek of it!" She said, grabbing her keys and trainers.

"So where to?" Hawa said.

"Let's go to a park."

We drove down to the park and got breakfast on the way. It was silent throughout the car journey and I could see that she was far from happy. When we finally arrived, I asked Hawa what happened.

"You can tell me." I said reassuring her. She seemed distant. Tears began rolling down her cheeks as she passed me her phone.
I couldn't believe it. This was low, even for Amar.

"He cheated?!?!??!?" I exclaimed.

"I know." She broke down into tears, and I just let her cry. I didn't say anything else. I know that this was something she had to let herself feel, otherwise she'd just block it out and make it worse. And I didn't want that for her.
"Hawa, he's not worth it. He really isn't."

She calmed down after a few minutes, and we continued in silence, until she spoke.

"I know that he's not worth it Dunya. But, the thing hurting me right now, is the belief I had in him. The belief that he had changed. I denied anything negative about him, and I chose to believe that he really had changed, and that too for the better. I just don't understand how I can be so weak?"

"Hawa, listen to me. If anything, you're not at fault here. You let your heart decide for you, and there's nothing wrong with that. I know that you were truly devoted to this guy, and he broke you once before, but you chose to forgive him. Do you realise how much strength it takes to forgive someone who hurt you? It takes so much. And it just goes to show just how much of a big heart you have. You chose to believe he's changed, because you always choose to see the good in people, and that's the most beautiful thing about you. You can never see someone through a negative light, there's always a positive thing about them for you. This is the same. Even though he hurt you beyond imaginable, you forgave him. You forgave him because your heart is so strong that it's capable of forgiveness. Do you realise how many people go through life without forgiving people? I consider that weak. But you? You're strong. You're so strong. And that's how I know, that you'll get through this, no matter how weak you might feel right now. You will get through this, just like you have previously."

I could see tears constantly scrolling down her cheeks, but I didn't stop her. I knew that she had to get these emotions out.

Her phone began to rang mid-conversation and I hurried to answer it.

"DON'T YOU DARE RING HER AGAIN" I shouted as loud as I could, and I must have said some other (not so nice) things to him.

Silence followed. And she began to laugh.
"Nice." She said.

"You're welcome." I said, blocking his number from her phone.

"All jokes aside Hawa. You've got me, and I won't let you go through this alone. So please understand that you are capable."

"… Also, PLEASE take this tissue because I'm starting to see things I don't want to."

"Haha, funny!" She exclaimed as she wiped her tears and her nose.

We drove back to hers that day, and majority of the time was spent in silence. I knew she was going to be this way for a while, and I didn't expect her to recover straight away. I just wish there was something I could do.. and then I realised, there was.. so I went home that day, and I went straight to my prayer mat.

"Ya Rab." I said, tears grasping at my eyes as I thought of the pain Hawa must be feeling right now.

"I know that this isn't it for her. I know that You have something greater planned. Just please help her see this too. Give her the patience to get through this. You're the only One I felt comfortable enough to turn to in my times of darkness and trials, and I hope that she does the same. I want her to feel the same peace that you allowed me to feel. I want her to be okay, without feeling like she needs someone to be okay. I want her to understand that love is not meant to hurt.. at least not like it has for her. Please, ya Rab.."

I ended my prayers that night, feeling as though my prayers are being listened to. I knew, in my heart, that Allah will see to Hawa getting back up from this.

I had to do a little more writing that night. There was a lot of things on my mind. I knew I had to, so I got my notebook and I began to write..

> "At times, I sit on the prayer mat, and I can't seem to think of things to ask God for. I'm not perfect, and neither is my life. But, at times I feel like I'm starting to feel a lot more content with things. At times, there's nothing I want more from God, but peace. So I sit there, and I wait. I wait until I'm ready to get back up and carry on fighting my way through the dunya. I know that somewhere along this spiritual journey, Allah allowed me to accept things for what they are and introduced me to this feeling of contentment. I've always been one to think negative about things, before they even happened.. but some days, I think twice. But then, other times. I'm·

too overwhelmed from emotions to speak. I cry. And I cry all the tears I have to cry. I ask God what this feeling is, and whether I'll ever be able to make sense of it. Why do I still feel as though there's something missing when I can't possible think of what it could be? Why do I still feel as though there's a pain in my chest that I don't know the reason for? I try, and I try my hardest when I do, to think positive and keep going when possible. But at times, I fall weak. And I feel like, I'm learning. That perhaps.. this is how life will continue to be? Maybe, this is something I'll have to fight for as long as I live. Maybe it's something that I'll always have at the back of my mind. They say that letting go of the past is hard, but not impossible. But tell me, how is it possible to let go off the past when it's a part of you that always seems to make it's way back to you. The worst thing is, when people talk about letting go, they are referring to people.. but in this case I'm referring to the old me. The old me that I don't want back. I'm starting to believe letting go isn't possible.. I don't want to go down this route again.."

I stopped writing. And I sighed. I felt myself slowly going back to the same mental space I was in, back in sixth form. I didn't want to go back there. But I feel as though, the last few months have been so heavy. So heavy to accept, so heavy on my mind, that I have nowhere to put this heaviness.. no where but my mind. And there's only so much my mind is able to hold. If I was to talk logically about the 'problems' I think so much about, they won't seem as bad. But, there's just something about my mind, that can't seem to understand this. That, not all negative things that happen are really negative. I can't seem to help myself understand. I just know that I really don't want to go back to feeling so negative. Feeling so overwhelmed. So broken. So lost.

A lot of people say that it's okay, to not feel guilty. But you cannot say and then expect. It's always easier said than done, right? Guilt. Guilt is what follows when you feel as though you're not doing your soul justice. As though, there's something within you telling you that you're doing it wrong, and it's wrong which is why you're feeling this way. I've always believed guilt is a bad thing. But is it really? Maybe the fact that I felt this guilt, was perhaps Allah telling me to try that little bit harder? Maybe it was His way of motivating me. I read somewhere once, that this guilt we feel is also a sign of mercy from Allah. And it seems to be crossing my mind more than ever lately. I feel guilty for feeling emotions I don't necessarily have control over. And a part of me just assumed, it could only mean that my prayers are somewhat working? But what was this conflict of emotions I was feeling? Maybe, I **was** becoming closer to my main goal. Maybe, my soul was becoming more aware of it's purpose, hence why it' was beginning to feel just how much of a burden this dunya is. Maybe.

I went to sleep that day, not feeling entirely content with myself. I still felt guilty for feeling this way, but parts of me were trying to convince me that this guilt doesn't have to be a bad thing. It doesn't.

9

I woke up as early as I could that day, and I allowed myself to lay in bed for a while before getting up. I tried so hard not to think about the thoughts I had on my mind last night, but they were bound to be present. They were there, was it not just a matter of ignoring them? I really wanted to talk to someone about this, and most times, I would confront Hawa and just tell her I'm not doing so great… but I know that this is the time she needed me to be the strongest. So I had to be strong, for her. I had to be her support, just like she's been mine for so long. I checked in with her more times than ever to assure that she's not alone. And tried to visit her more often. I know, that even though she wouldn't admit it, she was feeling lonely, and I didn't want her to. But I guess, it's something she had to go through to grow through.

———

It was mid march and it was nearing to the end of the university year. I didn't have much assignments left to complete, so I tried my best to do them in the time I was at home. It'd come to a point where I didn't feel as though I wanted to attend university. So I wouldn't. I'd stay at home and catch up on lessons through the one's the tutors would upload. It was going somewhat well, and I was getting away with it, until I received an email from one of my tutors asking to book me in for a tutorial.

I guess it won't be that bad? I thought to myself.

I went ahead and attended the tutorial, and it didn't seem so bad. But I also had a lecture that day. And I braved it enough to attend. But, being all alone and attending a lecture of more than 100+ students who probably know someone or another, wasn't easy. I tried to stay away from everyone and just do my own thing, but it's never easy. I was feeling more anxious than anything. And I could feel the loneliness. It was the worst feeling I felt in a while.. and that was saying something. I lasted about 20 minutes, before I packed up and left. I made my way home as soon as possible, to avoid any kind of panic, but it was inevitable after all the thoughts and feelings that came rushing to mind.

I went home that day and rushed to bed. All I wanted to do in those moments was pray. Pray to the only One capable of understanding. But I couldn't even do that.. so I took my notepad and I wrote..

> "I've talked myself out of happiness many times.. but why can't I seem to talk myself into it? Why can't I seem to take my mind away from this constant cloud of negativity that I feel? What will it take to finally feel.."

I stopped writing, as tears began to scroll down my cheeks. I rolled up my sleeves and placed my hands over the scars I've never been proud to call mine. And I kept thinking about them. I didn't want to. I didn't want to feel this way. I wanted it to stop.

I did what any child would do in their moments of weakness. I ran to my mother, and I hugged her.

"Dunya?" She said, sounding very concerned in her tone.

"Mum, I can't do this.."

"Do what..?"

"This.. life.."

"Dunya, what are you saying?"

I cried and I let myself cry all the tears I had to and I hugged onto her so tight in those moments. And I genuinely feel as though.. if I hadn't had my mother, I would not be here right now.. in these moments, writing what I'm writing now. I fell asleep in my mother's lap that night. And she let me. She didn't move me. She didn't wake me. She let me sleep.

The next morning, when I woke up, I knew I had to explain what had happened. But instead, I chose to remain quiet. I just didn't feel like I had the courage to explain.. especially when I didn't know what it was that I had to explain. How do you even tell someone you're feeling this, when you don't really know what 'this' is?

"Are you okay?" My mother said, as she passed me my tea.

"Yeah, I am."

"I don't think you are.. and I know you won't tell me.. so maybe you'll tell a doctor instead?"

"Mum-"

"It's really not up for discussion. You're going to the doctors Dunya. You really scared me last night, and I don't know what I'd do if you actually.." At this moment, she began to cry, and my heart sank.

I was the reason behind my mother's tears, and I don't think I'll ever forgive myself for this.

"Mum.. please don't cry. I'll go doctors I promise.."

I got up and got ready to go.. but I just couldn't shift this feeling of guilt I had. Was I being selfish for feeling this way? I blamed myself in those moments. I asked myself things, I don't think I've ever given myself the answers to. And I continued to spiral down this route of negativity. It felt never-ending.

I went to the doctors that day. But it didn't help in any way. In those moments, I just didn't feel like I wanted to accept help from others. I knew that if there was someone who could help me overcome this, it was myself. I had to do this for me. I had to understand that I wanted to move ahead. I had to do this alone. It was my battle to fight. It had to come from me.

So I tried once more.. I tried with all the strength I had left.. I tried.
I knew that I had to begin by allowing myself to turn back to some kind of normality, which meant finally braving the horrors of going to university and facing other people, even though I didn't want to. I knew that I wouldn't feel better if I kept on cooping myself up.
If anything, I kept the thought of my mum crying in the back of my mind and kept telling myself how much I didn't ever want her to feel that way because of me again.. so if everything else went to vain.. I had to do it for her. The one that brought me into this dunya, and brought me up with so much love.

Of course, I had to begin where my heart truly felt peace.. in sujood. I remember that night clearly. I remember the tears I shed, and the amount of times I begged Allah for some clarity for the way I was feeling. I remember asking Him to save me from myself, because it felt like I was almost becoming the poison I tried so hard to keep myself away from. I told Him how ashamed I was for feeling this way; but how I couldn't help it. I told him that I'd been trying, and I knew that He knew just how much I was trying.. but somewhere along the route of trying, I stopped trying as much. And I fell weak to my mind. I told Him that I felt as though my mind was winning against me, and it wasn't a good thing. I wanted it to be positive, but it wasn't that way. And I told Him to help me. I asked Him to find me, just like He found me previously. And this time, I asked to be found without getting so lost again. I prayed as long as I could that night and I didn't stop myself from crying. I didn't hold back my tears whenever I was in front of Allah, because I knew that in some way, it was Allah having mercy on me. There was once a time, where I felt as though crying was the weakest emotion a human could feel, but I've been coming to understand just how much strength lies in really expressing your emotions. And Allah allowed me to realise this through prayer, and for that I am consistently grateful. So I cry, and I express. Until there's no more tears left for me to physically shed, and the burden I carry no longer seems like it's weighing me down so much that I cannot move ahead. A lot of people talking about having a safe place, and for me, this was it.. the prayer mat.

I woke up the next day, and forced myself to get out of bed straight away. It might seem trivial for many, but for me, it was nothing short of an accomplishment. The only reason being, because my worst days I would spend in bed and wouldn't find the strength in me to get up and face the world. But I knew that if I wanted to try again, I had to begin somewhere, and so I began by getting up out of bed, and getting ready for the day ahead.. for whatever it may bring.

10

"DUNYA!" Hawa exclaimed as loudly as she possibly could, as I could feel my cheeks burning up and strangers eyes wondering towards us.

"Hawa.. we are in public!" I said, trying to get her to feel the embarrassment. But who was I kidding?

"Haha, like I care." She said, as she went in for a hug.

I told you.

We hadn't met for a few days, and the last time I saw her, she had just gotten her heartbroken for the second time, but now? She seemed okay. Not completely happy. Not completely broken. But okay. And I knew that feeling too well, so I knew I had to get her to understand that it was okay to talk about her feelings and not hide away.

"So, to what do I owe this pleasure Madam Dunya?" She said, as she began giggling.

"Erm.."

"Ooh - sounds serious." She said, as we finally found seats and sat down.

"I'm worried about you Hawa." I said.

I noticed how she lifted her head straight away and plastered on a fake smile.

"Honestly, why? I'm okay Dunya. I would tell you if I wasn't.."

"But that's the thing, I feel like you're not even allowing yourself to understand that you're not okay. I feel like you're not dealing with this heads on and you're letting it pile up.. and that can't be good.."

"I guess, I'm just trying to be more positive and not give it the thought or time of day.."

"But surely you understand that just by avoiding something, it doesn't go away, right?"

"Yeah, but.."

She looked down, and fell silent.

"Look, of course I don't want to see you in pain, but I also know that you're not letting yourself heal by trying to sugarcoat things and painting a smile over your wounds. I know you've always been the one that looks to positive outlooks rather than negative ones, but I really want the best for you Hawa, and I don't want you to end up like.."

I couldn't bring myself to say it.

"Like?" Hawa questioned.

It went silent for a minute.
She asked again.

"Dunya? Like what?"

"Like me.. I guess."

"Dunya, come on. Don't talk like that."

"But it's true Hawa. You've always been the one that's been open about your emotions and you've never hid anything from me. You've always dealt with things as they've come along, and you've faced your battles head on. You never hide away, not like I do. I spent so long trying to hide my true emotions, that I made it worse for myself to the point where I didn't feel like living. And I really don't want you to go down this route, because I've seen it first hand, and it's the worst. And I don't want you or even anyone else to experience this pain, because of how bad it hurts.."
I let out a sigh. And then I looked up to see Hawa tearing up.

"Dunya, I'm just.."

"It's okay, you can tell me Hawa.. I'm here." I went in for a hug and reassured her.

"Give me a few minutes.." She said.

"That's fine, take as long as you need."

"In the meanwhile can we eat, because I'm starving?" I said, trying to lighten the mood a little.

We ordered our food, and she didn't speak throughout. I didn't force her to speak, because I knew that she would talk to me. But I just wish I could have taken this pain she was feeling away from her.

"I'm ready." Hawa said, as she placed her fork on her plate, and looked at me.

"I'm listening.." I said reassuringly.

"Okay, so. I guess I'm not feeling as hurt because a part of me still believes that he will come back to me, and we'll try again, like he has previously. I still have hope in whatever this is on his behalf. I still believe that, there's some part of him that loves me. I still believe in the things he told me. And I keep going over everything in my head.. and just none of it makes sense. Surely, there must be a reason as to why Allah allowed him to come back into my life? Surely, in normal terms this means that he is the one, right?"

"Hawa. It's completely normal for you to feel like this. He's been such a big part of your life for so long, so it would be completely okay for you to feel like he's not leaving anytime soon. I know that you're finding it hard to accept because of how many times he's left and returned, but something you have to understand is that this time? The fact that he left? Didn't come from him, but from Allah.."

"What do you mean?" Hawa said, as she looked at me, trying so hard not to tear up.

"I mean. The first few times that he went and he returned, he was willing. Perhaps, Allah allowed him to return because, maybe, just maybe.. at that time, his intentions were pure, and he wasn't intending on hurting you. Perhaps, the lesson he was written to teach you, you had not yet learnt, so Allah allowed him to come back to you, in hope that you might learn it for yourself. But, then you were about to commit your entire life to this person.. the same person that hurt you so much previously. And perhaps, he just wasn't written for you. Perhaps, this isn't the kind of happiness Allah had in mind for you, so He removed him. And He removed him in a way, where you realise that your self worth isn't reliant on having another human being by your side, but by having yourself.. Perhaps, Allah allowed him to be removed in this way, because He knew that you had to finally let go, once and for all.."

"That makes sense Dunya, but how do I accept it?"

"It takes time Hawa. Accepting that someone isn't written for you, when all you've ever prayed for is for them to be yours, isn't something that is accepted overnight. It's an ongoing battle, but a battle that you have the strength to get through.. I just know that someone as beautiful hearted as you? Allah has an equally beautiful person written for you to spend your life with. And Amar wasn't it. He wasn't worthy of you. And I hope that what's happened, and this heartbreak helps you to understand this.. I really hope it does.. Allah saved you from marrying the wrong guy Hawa. He knows that you're worthy of someone better. Please trust His choice for you."

"I'll try to accept this Dunya.. I will.. but please bear with me, if some days.."

"Stop right there Hawa.. don't even think about apologising for being down or heartbroken, because I'll actually leave you right here and let you make your own way home.."

"Ooooh touchy." She joked, as we both giggled.

I knew she was strong enough to get through this, but I also knew that she shouldn't rush the process.

"So, can we go shopping now or?"

"Weren't you just saying the other day how you're trying to save money Dunya?" Hawa said, smirking.

"Yeah but, you know, money is there to be spent!" I said, trying to be as convincing as possible.

"That should be your motto, the amount of times you've said it!" She laughed.

We spent the remainder of the day shopping and trying on clothes. It felt like old times, and I felt proud of myself. But more than that, I felt proud of Hawa. The last year and so, has been hard on both of us, but I know that with each other, and with the help of Allah, we would get through this.. it was only a matter of time. We just had to keep going, no matter what got in the way.

Truth be told, I was feeling a lot more motivated after the day I had with Hawa. It allowed me to realise just how much I do want to live, and how wrong I was to think that I don't. I know that it was during a time where I couldn't control the thoughts that were racing on my mind, but I was able to realise it today. And I hoped that I wouldn't ever allow that thought to cross my mind again. I realised how I'm not alone, even though I might feel it at times. I felt inspired. So I did what I do best, and I took my notepad out, and I began to write..

"Sometimes, when you're at your lowest, you almost become stubborn. You allow yourself to believe that you don't want to turn to anyone, and you don't need anyone. You block yourself out from everyone and ensure that no-one gets close enough to hurt you more hurt than you are in that instance. But majority of the time, the only reason for why you're hurt, is because of yourself. It's because of the constant mind battles you've been having, and you become tired of fighting, so sometimes, it's like you just let it win. You let it win, and you let it convince you of things that you wouldn't otherwise think were true. It tells you that you're all alone, and you have no-one. And you believe it. No questions asked. It tells you that you're not worthy of happiness. And you

93

believe that too. Again, no questions asked. But this is the very cycle, that I've tried so hard to get out for so long. And at times, when things are going somewhat well in my life, I finally feel as though I have won. That I won't go back to feeling this way again. And then, it hits me out of nowhere. As though, it was something waiting to happen. Something that has always been there, and it just sort of creeps up on you every so often. I guess, my mental health is something like that. Although, at times I feel like I'm defeating all the negativity that lives in my mind, other times, I'm made to feel as though I haven't really defeated anything. And I guess, today, was one of those days where I realised that defeating it may not be entirely impossible. So, I'm willing to try again. And maybe again. And again after that. I'm willing to try as many times as it takes, to get myself to understand that I am far much stronger than the negativity my mind tries to drown me in. So here's to trying. Trying and not giving up."

I smiled as I wrote those last words: 'not giving up'. And I felt it within my heart, that I won't give up this time. That I won't give up until I am finally in the mental state I feel happiest. I mean, I had already taken a step towards feeling some normality by meeting Hawa and spending a day with her. And it had already helped. So what's not to say that trying to do other things that I would normally do, wouldn't help too? Although, I did feel this motivation, I also, at the back of my mind hoped that this motivation won't be weak, and it'll stay strong, no matter comes my way.

I woke up the next morning, and decided that it was time I faced going to university. It was a big step, but it was one of the things I had put off for so long, and I knew that I had to do this. I had to do it for my mind, more than anything.

So I got up and got ready. I made my way to university, by the usual form of transport I would take: bus. I just found bus journeys long, but peaceful. I would normally sit next to the window and just gaze out the window. I mean, we all do that don't we? We pretend like we're in some kind of movie. No? Just me then.

As I was lost in my thoughts, I heard the announcement, that my stop was coming up next. But then I realised, there was someone sat next me. When did this happen?

"Erm.. excuse me please?"

"So I guess you didn't have to practice this time?" He sounded familiar.

"Oh my.."

"Gosh?" He smirked.

"Erm.." I was startled.

I mean, he was charming, but I was seriously beginning to freak out. Like, okay, I've met him briefly once on this bus, but now again? Surely that can't mean..

"Yeah.. I'm not following you.. I swear." He said, laughing.

"I attend the same university. And this was the only empty seat.. you didn't put your bag down today, so I assumed you weren't saving it for anyone."

"Wait no.. I didn't mean to sound rude." I shot back, trying to be polite, and trying not to make it out like I was just wondering if he was actually following me.

"Are you going to move now or?" I asked, in the nicest way possible (at least it sounded nice to me).

"No." He said. Blocking the way, so that I was unable to get off the bus.

"No.. I mean seriously.. I'm going to be late.."

"Ask again?" He said, smirking.

"You're really enjoying this aren't you?" I said, getting a little annoyed at this point.

He carried on smirking.

"Ugh fine, can you please move.. PLEASE?"

"I guess I'll take that. Wow, aren't you a polite one!?" He said, as I walked past him and tried to ignore the sarcasm.

Normally, I'd be quick to say something back, but I really had 5 minutes to get to lecture, and I knew that could only mean one thing.. the best seats were taken. You know? The best seats were always the ones right at the middle. It's like you're not sat too close to the front so that you're able to use your phone without the lecturer knowing. And you're not sat so far back that the lecturer thinks you've just strolled in super late. I can't be the only one that thinks of these things. Or am I? Okay I'll stop.
I got to the lecture theatre, and to my surprise.. it was empty.

"What?!" I said to myself.

I sat in the middle of the lecture theatre, and waited a few minutes. But no-one showed.

"Am I dreaming?" I pinched myself.

I checked over my timetable again, just to make sure I was actually in the correct room, and I was. But where was everyone?
I was scrolling through my emails, before I heard that same voice again..

"No way!!"

I looked up to see the mystery guy from the bus.

"Okay, seriously. Now I MUST ask. Are you following me?"

"Haha please!" He exclaimed.

"I also do this course. And trust me, I'm as freaked out as you are with these constant meetings."

"Okay, enough of that. But seriously? Where is everyone???" I said, rapidly scrolling through my lecture forum to see if there was anything announced today.

"Erm, yeah, today's lecture was cancelled. Aren't you in the group chat?"

"No, I don't like those things."

"You don't like group chats…?"

"Yeah."

"Strange." He muttered under his breath, but I heard him quite clearly.

"You know what, I've actually come to university after quite a while, and it's taken quite a lot for me to actually come here, and you're really NOT helping. I really thought I would be making some kind of step today only to find out that this stupid lecture is cancelled and I just.."

I began to panic, as tears streamed down my face.

"Hey. I'm sorry."

"Will you just GO already!?" I said, almost screaming.

I heard him walking away.
I tried to gather myself by focusing on my breathing and repeating the same thing over and over again. Whenever I was in huge distress, I had a habit of whispering these words: "Allah please help, please." I kept on doing this, until I felt somewhat okay. It was kind of my strength. That whenever I felt somewhat weak, or somewhat down, I would think of Allah straight away. I couldn't think of anyone better to ask for help from. He was always there. He was always listening and I knew this. So I wouldn't stop talking to Him, even when I was away from the prayer mat. It was the only thing that kept me going.

A few moments later, and I had finally calmed down. I wiped my tears, and reached out to get my water bottle, but as I reached for my bag, I noticed him sitting on a seat a few rows above me.
He looked at me, with concern on his face. He then mouthed the words: "are you okay?" And then pointed towards me and showed me his thumb.

I didn't know what to think at this point. What were these constant meetings? Why did he feel like a stranger but also feel so familiar at the same time?

"I'm sorry." I said. As I gathered my things and tried to get up to leave.

"Sorry?" He asked, as though he didn't know I owed him an apology for snapping at him.

"Yeah, for snapping at.."

"You're not going to be apologise for something that wasn't your fault, are you? I mean, surely that should be one of your steps?" He said, with genuine kindness in his words.

I looked up at him, and I smiled.

"You're right. I'm not sorry. You deserved.."

"Ohhkaaaayyy, moving on.." He said, laughing.

We got to talking that day. And he told me about his mental health. He had recently began his journey in trying to recover from depression. He told me how he was on anti-depressant medication for a while, and how it made him feel even worse once he stopped taking them.

"I'm sorry you felt that way.."

"Are you apologising again?" He said, raising his eyebrow at me.

"Haha, okay.. but seriously.. you're so strong for going through all that, and still not giving up.."

"I am strong. But I also believe that anyone who goes through mental health difficulties, no matter how they deal with them.. is strong. I guess, the biggest step for me was accepting that I won't always have good days, where I'm trying my best to tackle my mental health heads on. Some days? I won't feel like doing anything that helps myself and my mind. I won't feel like being proactive in achieving my 'steps'. But that's okay, because my bad days don't mean that I'm going backwards. It just means that I'm still on this journey, and I'm still learning. And I guess, a part of me believes, I'll always be learning. There's just so much that it teaches you, right? It teaches you, that in the end, it really is just you, and you need to be okay with that."

"You're right." I said.

"Sometimes, I think the whole point of trials like these are because Allah is trying to prove that we are worthy of receiving the love we give others. We are worthy of self-love. We deserve it just as much as anyone else."

We both sat there in complete silence for a few minutes.

"So, I think I'm gonna go see my lecturer now, as I have a tutorial." I spoke, as I got up.

"Yeah, that's fine. But before you go.." He stopped talking all of a sudden and looked down.

"My name is Dunya." I said, as I walked away.

I walked in to the room where my lecturer was sat, and took a seat, as she told me to.

"Before, I begin, I must ask.. are you okay?" She said, looking concerned.

"Yeah, why?" I said, smiling.

"Your attendance has become quite a concern, and we were afraid that you were losing motivation, or perhaps something else? But whatever it is, I'd just like you to know that there's people at university who are willing to support you.." She said, as she passed me a leaflet on mental health.

"If ever, there's something that's come up, please don't be afraid to ask for extra time on assignment deadlines." She paused.

"Thank you Lisa. I guess, although it's been overwhelming trying to deal with my mental health, I haven't really required an extension." I spoke, as to not give so much away, but to also prove that I wasn't just 'skiving'.

"I understand." She said, facing me, and placing her pen down on her desk. She looked at me for a few seconds with understanding in her gaze, as she said:

"It's just, I know, first hand just how hard it is to be in your position. I too went through mental health difficulties at university, which almost caused me to drop out. It can be hard trying to express what it is that makes you feel a certain way, and so you choose to just hide away in hope that it won't last long and you'll be able to get back to 'normal' soon. But, I guess, the biggest battle lies in accepting that your mental health is a part of you that you must carry, no matter how heavy. On the heavier days, it'll be hard, but the strength you've built throughout will help you along the way. You must remember something though.. you're not alone, no matter how alone you might feel."

I looked at her and nodded my head, because I genuinely didn't think anyone would understand the struggle, but maybe I was wrong.

"You're right, and honestly, it's something that I'm working on." I said, as I got my books out in order to talk to her about the assignment.

"Good, I'm glad. I'm glad you battled through and managed to come into university today."

"Yeah, about that. A little heads-up about the cancellation would have been great." I said, smirking.

"I'll make sure to send an email and not text next time!" She said smiling.

I was actually quite relieved as to how supportive Lisa was that day, and honestly? It felt like a huge burden had been lifted, knowing that if need be, she understands. So I guess, it allowed me to understand that perhaps coming into university wasn't really scary. Not as scary as my mind was making it out to be anyways.

I spent the rest of the day at university working through missed lecture notes, and trying to plan my assignments. But I kept on getting distracted with the conversations I've been having that day. They just felt so wholesome, and I wondered if this was Allah proving to me that, if I try, then I can get to where I want to be.

I went home that day and caught up on my prayers. As I was making dua, he kept coming to mind. I was thankful for the insight he gave with his advice, and genuinely wished him well. But why was I thinking of him at this point? I read somewhere once, that when you think of someone during dua, it probably means you should pray for them. So I did. I prayed for him, and asked Allah to make his trials easier. But what was this feeling? I really couldn't shake it. I felt odd. I was never like this. I was never interested in talking to guys, because I knew how wrong it was. But, this just seemed.. okay?
I knew that I had to somehow try to make sense of these feelings, so I got my notepad out and I began to write.

"It's strange isn't it? How, sometimes, you meet someone, and you just click. You don't try. No efforts involved. And yet they understand you. And somewhere during the conversations you have, you almost feel as though they understand you too well.. It almost feels like you're reuniting with a soul you've met previously, only you haven't.. I.."

"Wow." I said to myself, as I decided to stop writing and just leave that entry incomplete.

I went to sleep that day feeling somewhat at peace. I had this renewed faith that Allah is answering my duas and He will make it all okay, it's just a matter of time.

A few weeks later, and I had already become used to a daily routine. I would get up before sunrise and pray Fajr, before eating breakfast and leaving for university.

I knew that I had to somehow make up for the months that I lost out on my studies, and I knew that it was almost the end of the semester so I had to ensure I passed this year, in order to successfully enter year 2.

I had seen him around a lot. I still didn't know his name. But he asked me how I was at times, and I replied with 'Alhamdhulillah'. I didn't ask how he was, but I hoped that he was. At times, he would be sat in the silent computer room opposite me, doing his own thing as I was typing away. I tried not to give it much notice, but it somehow felt normal? I was trying my best not to talk to him as much, because I knew, by looking at Hawa's story, just how much attachments can hurt. How much hold they can have over you. I feel as though, it's the only reason he perhaps didn't try to force conversation, because he knew too. I guess, a part of me hoped that we could talk, but I knew just how wrong it would be, and how much hurt it might lead to. So I didn't. But I did, what I do best, and I prayed for him instead. I asked Allah to help me make sense of these feelings and to guide me to become the best version of me, without feeling as though I need someone to do that for me. I asked Him to take care of him, and to guide him too.

I was meeting Hawa today after university, as it was the last day that I was required to attend, and I hadn't seen her in a while as I tried to keep myself busy with catching up with my education.

As I walked up to her, she had this look. She was squinting and then all of a sudden, she smiled and came running up to me.

"Is this normal? I'm not so sure with you!" I said, laughing as we hugged.

"I should be asking you that."

"And, what could you possibly mean by that?" I said, looking at her, interested in knowing what she was going to come out with now.

"You've met someone.."

I swear I didn't mention anything? How did she know?

"Your silence kind of gives it away Dunya. WHO IS HE!?"

"Hawa, chilllll." I said, grabbing her hand and walking.

"It's nothing like that.." I continued, as her smile kept on getting bigger (if that was even possibly because she was BEAMING with happiness at this point). "I met him that day when I came to see you after university. Well, not met, but we crossed paths. And I didn't think I'd see him again. But he was on the same bus as me again, so we of course crossed paths again. And I realised he attends the same university and does the same course as me.."

"Do continue." She said, giggling.

"But, it's not what you think. I haven't really talked to him much.. Well apart from.." I paused.

"But that doesn't matter, we don't even talk. It's not even something to be so ecstatic about Hawa, seriously, you're such a drama queen!"

"… Are you going to continue or do I have to sweeten the deal and buy you dessert first?"

"Well, that would help." I said, as I walked ahead into my favourite dessert shop.
We ordered our desserts and I could just tell she was eager for me to continue speaking.

"Okay, okay, calm your horses, I'll tell you."

"It kind of feels strange to say this out loud, but I genuinely feel like we have some kind of bond? Like the one time we actually spoke, it was about mental health. And he was so understanding. And I just felt this thing in my stomach, I don't know what it was.."

"Sweetie" Hawa said, as she put her fork down, and grabbed my hand.

"Normal people call those BUTTERFLIES." She began to laugh.

I couldn't help but laugh too, as I continued telling her about how we would cross paths but not talk, but somehow it felt comfortable being in his presence.

"But, Hawa.."

"I know, I know. You don't want to get hurt.."

"You're right, I don't. I just feel like there's just so much hurt I've had to deal with, that came from myself, that I cannot imagine what I would do, if someone else hurt me.."

"But, must every situation that includes attachments, lead to hurt?"

"It's kind of the reason that Allah prevents us from being so attached to worldly things, right? Even if that's to people too.."

107

"I get you, but perhaps, this can work out in a 'halal' way." She said, actually being serious in her tone.

"What do you mean?"

"I mean, what if you two are meant to get married?"

I began to laugh, as I said: "Oh come on Hawa, don't be so naive. I'm sure there's got to be more to this. There's so much thought and understanding that's got to be between two people, in order for them to even contemplate marriage. And I don't even know his name.."

"You know what Dunya? I'm not even going to ask.. but please continue." She said, smirkingly eating her ice-cream.

"I just don't even want to think of the possibilities of him being in my future.. imagine, he isn't? Won't that hurt?"

"Of course. I understand you 100%. But I know, and I can for a fact that you are praying for him."

"Okay, are you living in my mind now?" I said as I rolled my eyes at her and scoffed.

"Make fun of it as much as you want, but for real.. there's something about you that just gives it away. It's like you've found a new purpose.. and maybe you're not pursuing it, but you know it's there.. I feel as though, deep down, you're hoping it'll turn into something more, and so you're praying for it to happen the right way. You're praying, because you don't want to feel as though you've gone into something else that could possibly be the reason you're led to more pain that you've only inflicted on yourself."

"Is this really coming from my Hawa? I'm so proud of how smart and wise you've become."

"I guess I've learnt from the best? But also, I've learnt through things Allah has sent me. That being wise is the only way to be." She said, as we both giggled away and kept on talking, until we realised how late it had gotten, and rushed to get home.

I fell asleep that day, knowing that there was truth in what Hawa was saying. I knew, that she knew, but I was perhaps too afraid to even admit it. But I knew, that if I wanted it to happen the right way, I would have to pray to Allah, and trust in His timing and His plan. So that's what I continued to do.

12

I got up that morning and received the notification that my assignments were ready to collect. I would always have to submit both paper and online copies... no idea why, don't ask. I decided to go into University and perhaps look around and see if I can manage to borrow some books to read over the holidays. Now that I was free from assignments and uni deadlines, I was hoping to read and just immerse myself in a book. The feeling of reading a new book.. ah, there's nothing like it!

I prayed before I went. And as usual, I sat on the prayer mat, just a little while longer. I would just sit there and feel the peace. It was my safe place, and at times I didn't want to leave. So I would stay as long as I needed. But I knew that I had to get to university and back by the time it gets late. So I got up from the prayer mat, folding it carefully and placing it on my sofa. As I was doing this, I saw my mum looking at me from the door.

"Ma sha Allah." She said, with a big smile on her face.

"I'm so proud of you Dunya." She brought me into a hug, and proceeded to place her hand on my face.

"You've come so far from where you used to be, and recently it shows. Not just in what you do, but in how you are. Alhamdhulillah you seem a lot more at peace.. May Allah keep you happy always, Ameen."

"Ameen.. thank you mum. But are you planning on making me cry just as I'm meant to leave for university?" I said, letting out a little giggle.

"Of course not! See you in the evening in sha Allah.' She said, as she walked me out to the door. She would always do this thing 'where she'd watch me walk out. I didn't know how to describe it, but it made me feel as though she was doing dua, and with my mothers duas? I felt protected. As though, there's nothing that could possibly hurt me.

Throughout my journey to university, I was gazing outside the bus window (as you do), and wondering.. and he came to mind. I hope he's okay. I pray that his mental health is okay. I hadn't seen him much recently, and I kind of got worried? Was that weird?

"Come on Dunya!" I whispered to myself. Was I getting attached to someone that probably isn't promised to me? I couldn't help but wonder all these thoughts. But I knew, that I had to do what I do best.. and ask Allah to help me make sense of it all. I mean, surely I wouldn't feel this way had there not been something more?

"The bus will be terminating at the last stop." The bus driver announced, which instantly woke me from my thoughts.

I proceeded to walk towards University, and you'd never guess who I saw? Saha.

She was smiling at me as though we were friends, and I didn't know what that meant, but it felt odd, for one.. She proceeded to walk towards me and began to speak.

"Hey stranger!" She said

"Stranger?" I said, trying not to sound too annoyed.

"Yeah.. I mean you never hang with us anymore."

"Wasn't I clear the first time we all hung out? I really don't want negativity.. Did you need something?"

"Just wanted to ask how you are.. and.."

"And?"

"And I wanted to apologise. I realise how abrupt I was in the way I treated you.."

"It's okay, I forgave you a long time ago."

"If you forgave me, then why don't you come say hi?"

"I forgave you, but that doesn't mean I want that negativity in my life again. I'd prefer to just remain by myself. This is the time for me to focus on any studies, not worry about pleasing others or making friends."

"I agree.."

"I'll see you around I guess." I said, as I proceeded to walk off.

Truth be told, it was the first time she was apologising for the way she acted. But I had forgiven her a long ago, because I knew that I was better off without this burden weighing me down. The thing is, when someone does you wrong and you don't receive an apology from them, you make yourself understand that holding onto the negativity and everything attached to them, is not worth it. I mean, no-one really owes us an apology. It's just something we feel as though we are owed when they hurt us. Of course, it's the courteous thing to do, but not everyone will. And I allowed myself to accept this. I realised that it was better to forgive than to feel as though they owe me something. It was kind of like a method that allowed me to move on from a lot of things, you know? Like, I wouldn't give it much thought after I taught myself to forgive them.

I received my results and went to the silent computer room, so that I can read through the feedback and make notes on things I could perhaps improve on. As I was reading through them, I heard someone coughing. I looked up, and it was him.
I gasped. I didn't want to say anything, but at the same time, I did?

"You sound ill.."

"Oh.. just a little cold." He said, smiling.

He was always smiling. I liked that. It reminded me of how I would be at times. How even though I was battling things, I would still smile.

I didn't say much after that, but I could see him looking over at me. And there came a point, where we both locked eyes. But I instantly, looked down. This feeling.. It was so.. It was odd.
I got my notebook out, and I tried to make sense of it, by writing.. and I saw the previous piece of writing that I started but didn't finish.. was Hawa right?

> "Soul mates. I always wondered what it meant by soul mates. I used to think how it can be physically possible to meet someone, and feel as though they weren't a stranger. I used to think it wasn't possible. But why do I feel as though he's my soul mate? Why do I feel as though his timing in my life was nothing short of a blessing? The thing is, there's a lot of things that have happened, and there have been days where I haven't really felt so great, but somehow? I keep going. And I feel as though, I have a bigger purpose now. And every time I proceed to think about the future, somehow, he's there? I get that some might say its crazy. I mean I still don't know his name. But there must be a reason for these feelings, for his entry into my life, for this mutual understanding we have. The kind of

understanding that doesn't always require words. That's rare. It really is. And I can honestly say, I've never felt this way about anyone.. ever. So why now?"

I kept reading over what I wrote, and most times that I would read over it? I would smile. But also? It was as though there was this fear of getting myself hurt creeping into my mind. And I know that previous to this, every time I felt somewhat overwhelmed, it would lead to panic. But I was getting better at controlling the urge to go fully into panic mode. Most times, I would close my eyes, and just imagine I'm talking to Allah. I would remind myself of my safe place, and I would even go there, if it got too much. At times, I would let myself cry, but not so much that I couldn't control my breathing. I guess, it was progress? It was finally as though I was allowing myself to understand that crying is okay. It's okay to cry. Emotions are there to be felt. There's no use in hiding them away, and then letting them pile up until the point where you just can't control it.

I finally gathered the confidence to look back up. I saw that he had his earphones in, and was typing away. I was quick to look away. I finished my work, and gathered my belongings to leave. As I was doing this, I saw that he was following suit.

"Bus?" He asked.

I nodded my head, and proceeded to leave. He followed.
He wasn't helping. I was as confused as ever, and I hoped that Allah would answer me. So I knew that when I got home, that's the first thing I would do.. go to the prayer mat and talk to Allah.

That night, I spent quite a long time just sitting and talking to Allah. At times, I would fall short of words, but I knew that He knew what I felt. So I let my heart speak for me. For once, I wasn't awake so late, with pain seeping through my every thought. This time? I just needed His guidance. I needed to know. I needed to know that these feelings weren't there for no reason. I wanted to know why they were so strong. So I kept talking to Him about what I felt and I kept asking Him for some insight. And I knew that He would answer me. I just had to be patient. And during this patience, I knew I couldn't hope as much as I was. I knew that this hope would hurt me.

After praying, I got my notebook out, and I proceeded to write.

"Hope. Hope is a weird thing isn't it? It's like during the process of hoping, all you feel is happiness. You allow yourself to hope everything you've ever associated with happiness, and you don't stop. You don't stop hoping. It's like, ever since I've met him? I've felt this hope. Even if it was for the little things. At times, I would hope that I would see him again. Other times, I hoped that he would talk or say something. But then comes the inevitable.. the negativity attached to hope. Most times? It would scare me that I was hoping so much for someone I barely knew, yet I felt as though I had known him longer than I had known myself. It felt as thought our souls had already met, and it felt nothing short of a reunion. Hope. Hope is what's carrying me through at the moment. But I also don't want it to be the only thing helping me get through this. I don't want to hope so much that I lose myself in this hope. I mean, what if I'm hoping but I get hurt? Nothing is certain, and I need to remind myself of that. Nothing will be certain unless Allah has written it to be. So, I guess, all I can hope.. all I can pray for is that this is written. Because if it isn't, I cannot begin to imagine the pain I've driven myself towards. And I don't want this hope to be the reason I fall into this mental battle, even deeper than I was before..

I guess for once I'm hoping, but a part of me is believing too. Believing that there's more to this. More to us.."

"Wow." I sighed. I didn't read over it this time. I didn't think it would flow as I just let every thought out onto paper. But it was needed. I needed to write so that I can somehow understand these feelings that left me confused as ever.

I heard my phone ring, and it was Hawa. We would try to talk daily, as much as possible, and most times we wouldn't talk, but it just felt normal having her on the phone.
"Hey girl!" She said, sounding as chirpy as ever.

"Hey Hawa." I said, trying not to make it sound like I was thinking.

"What's wrong?" She instantly knew.

"Huh?" I asked.

"You seem a bit off. Are you okay?"

"Yeah.. I guess.." I said, turning the pages of my notebook.

"Have you been writing?"

"I have.. but for once? I've written and it still doesn't make sense."

"What is it? You can tell me."

"It's just, I have this hope and I'm kinda scared, but I've never hoped as much as I am right now. It's weird.."

"Dunya, it's normal to hope. It's human. We always expect things from this dunya. It's a part of our nature to do so. If we didn't hope, if we didn't expect, we wouldn't hurt. And if we didn't hurt, then we wouldn't be in this world.."

"I agree.." I said, somewhat understanding.

"I just hope it turns out good for you, whatever it is Dunya. I have a feeling I know, but I also don't want to say it. But I'll pray for you, and I guess the most you can do, is pray too. And just trust that whatever Allah has planned for you will happen."

"Thank you Hawa." I said, before asking her how she's doing and going about our daily talks.

I fell asleep, thinking about the day and trying to remind myself off something I was proud of that day. I was proud of myself for not panicking when I felt so overwhelmed. It was these little affirmations before bed that were helping me go on longer. And I fell asleep that night, knowing, believing that whatever was meant to happen, will happen.

13

The summer was finally among us.. but I still didn't know what I felt. A part of me wanted to be at university.. and the only reason being was to see him. Yeah… I still don't know his name. I hoped he was okay. Truth be told, I often thought about him a lot. I still didn't want to give these feelings a name though. I knew that once I did, I would be putting myself at risk of getting hurt. And I didn't think that would be a wise thing to do.

I would often distract myself with talking to Hawa and catching up on life with her. But it was present in the back of mind, and I didn't know how to just paint over it as though it means nothing to me… especially as I knew now that it did.

Most times though? I would sit on the prayer mat and I would talk to Allah. At first, I felt nothing short of ashamed, but why would I not talk to the one that knows the matter of my heart? Surely, He understands. Surely He's the only that will help me to understand.

I also made it a habit of mine to wake up before Fajr and pray Tahajjud. It just helped. Helped in ways, nothing has ever helped before.

"Ya Rab.." I said. I sat down as I finished my last rakat.

"Ya Rab.. what is this feeling?" I held my hands up. My heart felt uneasy. I had a lot of thoughts on my mind. Too many thoughts.

"Ya Rab.. help me. Guide me to the truth. Help me make sense of this, like you've helped me before. Ya Rab.." I began to cry. I thought of the times I tried so hard to guard this heart of mine from letting it attach itself to anyone.. to anyone not promised to be mine.

I continued.

"Ya Rab, please don't attach my heart to that which is not meant to be mine. Ya Rab. Save me from giving it to the wrong one.."

I sat on the prayer mat in silence after this. I didn't think I had much more to say. My tears would often speak for me, and I would feel at peace knowing I didn't have to speak.. because He understood.

I would sit on the prayer mat after praying for a while. It was my safe place, and the only place that truly felt at home. Especially because it seemed as though my heart was busy travelling. No idea what the destination is. No idea what route it would take. I just knew it was breaking away from the walls I tried so hard to build around it, and it was starting to flee from my control. I was scared. But more than that? I was ashamed. And I didn't know how not to be. I didn't know how not to feel this.

"Dunya?" My mum spoke. I didn't hear her come into my room, but I was startled to say the least.

"Yeah mum?" I said, getting up from my prayer mat and folding it.

"Why are you awake at this time? Are you having difficulty sleeping? I've been hearing you awake at this time for a while now.."

"Aw Mum.. it's nothing to worry about. I'm just praying." I said, walking up to hug her.

"Okay.. but promise me you'll tell me if somethings up? Or try to talk to me at least?" She asked, concern starting to become apparent in her tone.

"Of course. Now go sleep, I'll see you later in sha Allah.." I said.

She looked at me for a good minute, before she proceeded to walk out the room and close the door behind her.

They say that mothers have instincts. And I wondered. I wondered if she knew? I hope she didn't, though. Even though, I didn't really speak to him, I still felt guilty, as though I was doing something wrong by feeling this way. But I knew, I knew that I just had to trust God. I just had to wait it out and wait for Him to answer my prayers. It was just a matter of time.. I just had to be patient.. but oh how hard patience was at a time like this.

I did what I do best, and I got out my notepad.

> "Patience. Why does no one ever speak about how hard patience can be? I mean, every time we go through certain trials, we're told we just need to be patient. But, in those very moments when negativity is all that clouds your mind.. you can't be patient. It's not possible.."

I paused.. why was I beginning to become more negative again?
I crossed out what I wrote. I closed my eyes for a few minutes. I took a few deep breaths. And, I began again.

> "Patience. Truth is, patience is what we are told to have when we're going through trials. But patience isn't always easy. But I guess, nothing in this dunya is easy right? Otherwise it wouldn't be known as the testing place. You know how sometimes we feel as though we need guidance? We need help through a certain trial? Perhaps in the form of comforting words or just a shoulder to lean on? Sometimes, we want nothing more but for them to say: "it'll be okay." But truth be told, when do they to tell us? Most of us find it hard to believe. And it's normal I guess. I've always thought it's because we don't really find ourselves trusting that they know what

will happen.. because no one can know what will happen in the next few seconds let alone months or years.. apart from Allah. So now? Whenever someone talks to me about patience. I try not to rely entirely on their understanding of it. But rather? I turn to the Quran. To the words of Allah. And I remind myself to be patient over what befalls me (Qur'an 31:17). I remind myself to seek comfort in patience and prayer (Qur'an 2:153). And I tell myself that these words? They haven't come from humans. They have come from the One who knows. The One that knows exactly what will happen. The One that knows exactly what fruits will blossom from this patience. So, I talk myself into trusting that it'll be okay. I trust that He will make everything make sense.. some day. So I practice patience, as far as possible. But I guess? It's not always easy. At times I doubt myself. I think, am I not trusting Him enough? Why am I doubting what He has said? Surely He's never wrong. At times? It becomes hard to force myself to be patient. But deep down, my heart knows that I have to. I have to, because He has promised that He is with those that are patient. And that's all I want. That's all I need. For Him to be with me always. Always.."

Somewhere amongst writing those words. I felt tears falling down my cheeks. I didn't stop them. I let myself cry. I knew I had to.

I went to sleep that night, turning for about an hour or two. I couldn't seem to get my mind to stop. It was like a never ending spiral of thoughts. One that wouldn't just rest. One that perhaps didn't feel like it needed to rest because it had been crowded for too long.

It was 9AM and my phone was vibrating constantly. I had probably just fallen asleep an hour ago, but I had to somehow silence my phone. I looked to see who it was: "No Caller ID."

"Hello?" I answered, sounding half asleep and confused as to who would be ringing me.

"Hello, this is Saha.."

"Oh. What's up?" I asked, beginning to feel annoyed.

"Just wanted to ask if you received the news about the work experience fair? I know you're not in the group chat, so thought I'd ask or let you know.. it's today." She said.

At this point, I was beginning to feel guilty for pushing her away.. was I in the wrong for wanting to protect myself?

"Oh.. that sounds interesting. What time is it?" I asked, slightly easing my tone.

"1pm. I'll be going, so I'll see you there?" Saha asked.

"Yeah sure.. see you later.." I said, hoping to perhaps get a couple more hours of sleep in before having to head out.

It was a nice summer day today. The sun was shining bright, and parts of me were happy to see the arrival of beautiful weather. But most parts were still adamant on holding onto the negativity. I hoped that perhaps going out to university and distracting myself would help ease my pain. A part of me hoped that I would also see him..

I walked into university, trying to walk around the crowds to find a quiet place. And then I saw Saha. She was with her friends, so I didn't think of approaching her. I was thankful for her thinking about me and telling me about this fair, but at the same time, I knew that I had to be careful. Careful as to not allow myself to feel like I have company, especially after how it worked out previously.

I was reading a leaflet when I heard someone approach me.

"DUNYA!" She reached in for a hug.
Was I in some sort of parallel universe? Why was she being so nice?

"Hey.. Sahaa. Thank you for telling me about this, it's really useful." I smiled.

"No problem. I hope we can talk more.."
I smiled at her and was about to talk before I realised her friends walking towards us.

I began to think.. was there some sort of ulterior motive here? What if she was being kind for someone in return? *No Dunya, stop. Stop thinking.*

I continued to browse through the information leaflets, and try to ignore that they completed ignored any existence and began talking anyways. But then they began to whisper.. flashbacks.

"Ask her then Saha." A friend of hers said, probably for the tenth time.
I looked up instantly.

"Ask what?"

"Oh nothing.. you guys stop!" Saha said giggling.

"No, please go ahead.." I said, intrigued but also feeling as though panic was brewing within me. It was strange because I hadn't felt such panic for a while.

"Erm.. well.. there's this thing.." Saha said, grabbing my arm and pulling me to a side.

"You know that guy you always hang around with?"

She must be talking about bus-boy… but what about him?

"I mean I hardly hang around with anyone.. but yeah, I know who you're speaking about.. What about him?" I asked, thoughts racing through my mind.

"Well.. I kind of like him.." My heart dropped. But why? Why did it drop. Why did it feel like it broke in that instant? What did I expect, for a guy I hardly talk to, to wait around for someone that has never bothered to make conversation? What was happening. *Dunya stop.*

"Oh, that's cool.." I said.

"Why are you telling me though?"

"Well.. do you have his number…?" So there was an ulterior motive. I can't even say that I was shocked. But this was low.

"So this was your motive then? And there was me thinking you just wanted to show how sorry you were.." She began to roll her eyes.

"I don't know his number. Ask him." I said, as I pointed towards him walking towards us.

I began to walk away because I couldn't come to terms with what had just happened. I couldn't believe the emotions I had just felt. Why did I feel… jealous? There was nothing between us.. well nothing concrete.. we would

126

hardly even talk. So why? Why am I feeling like something is being taken away from me, something that wasn't even mine?

"Dunya?" He said, as he stopped walking and saw me walking away.

I ignored him. I had to somewhere quiet right now and this place filled with people wasn't it. I rushed to find an empty room. And I sat down.
I sighed. I tried so hard. So so hard, to not cry. But I had to. So I let the tears fall. I didn't stop them. I thought I could handle it.. but then I began to panic. I hadn't panicked in a while, and I thought I was getting used to not doing so. But I guess, I felt overwhelmed with everything I felt and all that happened today.

I began to pace my breathing out. Holding my hands tightly together and just whispering to myself: "Ya Allah.. please.."

I got my phone out, and dialled Hawa's number. But I couldn't bring myself to ring her. What had gotten into me all of a sudden? So many thoughts. So many feelings. And that too, all at once.

"Dunya?" It was him.

"It's okay Dunya." He said, walking towards me and handing a water bottle.

I looked down, and tried to just ignore him. But he wasn't letting me. He stood there, looking at me.
He sighed as he walked away but didn't leave the room. He took a seat on the chair on the other side of the room.

We sat in some sort of silence for about 10 minutes. And throughout that time I kept whispering to myself, the same thing.

"Ya Allah, please.."

I finally calmed down and my breathing seemed as though it was back in my control. I reached out for the water bottle, and I saw him looking at me. He seemed upset. But why? I wanted to ask. But I didn't.

"Are you okay?" He spoke, after a minute.

"Ye.."

"Don't even think about lying.." He interrupted.

"I don't get it." I finally said.

"Get what?"

"Get why you're talking to me. Why this is happening. Nothing is making sense. I came into university as a way of distracting myself. But you're here too. And I got tracked into coming really but that's beside the point. I feel stupid." I was beginning to panic. Again.

"Dunya.. please. Don't cry. Just drink some water and try to remember that coming into university is still a step right? You didn't feel okay so you knew you had to do something.. and you did. You built courage to leave your home. To come into university. To face people who haven't seen in a while.."

"Don't." I said. I picked up bag as a way for me to leave. And he came and stood in the way.

"Please.. don't.." I said, a tear escaping my eyes.

He then moved out the way, and I walked out the room.

I found my way into the silent computer room, and got my notebook out. I furred it would be the only way I could make sense of these feelings.

> "Truth be told. I've spent majority of life, being careful. Trying to step away from people. Trying to back away whenever I feel as though I am getting attached. But why can't I seem to back away from him? He's everywhere. In my thoughts, in my duas, everywhere. I can't seem to stop thinking about him, no matter I do. What have I got myself into? I've always believed that attachments is what leads to pain. Attachments to the world. Attachments to people. And I've tried so hard not to become attached. But it's not that easy. At least that's what I've learnt. Attachments are not created with our permission. Sometimes it just happens.."

I stopped. I turned the page.

> "Sometimes, somewhere, you meet someone. And it feels right. But there's parts of you that can't accept that it may be right. Truth be told, many of us spend most of our lives trying to hide away. Trying to do what we can to protect ourselves from hurt. I mean, it's the normal human thing to do right? Growing up, whenever we experience pain, whenever we feel heartbreak, it's always linked to the emotions we let things and people hold over us. We assume that if we stop, that if we stop letting things hold importance in our lives, then we won't feel pain. But it's life. And that's okay. This life is not perfect. This life will never be perfect, so how can we try for something that is impossible? Hurt is inevitable. Attachments are inevitable. We can't spend our entire lives in solitude, because we feel as though people will hurt us. We can't do that because who said we can't hurt ourselves?"

I stopped writing again. I didn't know where I was going with this.. but in some ways, I managed to receive a definite answer. I was attached. And that too, to someone I don't even know is promised to me.

I got my phone out again, and I dialled Hawa's number.
It rang once and she answered.

"Heyyyyyy girl!" She said, in her cheery tone.

I didn't reply for a few seconds.

"OH no.. what's wrong Dunya?" She asked.

"I don't know Hawa." I said.

"Can we please meet today? I really need it." I asked.

She agreed, and told me to stay at university so that she can drive there and collect me.

I spent the next hour or so sitting and just reflecting. But whereas reflection is often peaceful.. this wasn't.

I received a text from Hawa saying she was outside. So I gathered my things and walked down the stairs towards the exit.
As I was walking towards the exit, I saw him. But he wasn't alone.
He was with Saha. And they were talking.
I looked at them, and then instantly looked away. My heart kept sinking that day, and I didn't know how to stop it from feeling this way.

I walked up to Hawa's car, and got in. But as soon as I saw her? I couldn't help but cry.

"Dunya???" She said, bringing me in for a hug.

"I feel so stupid Hawa."

"It's okay Dunya." She said reassuringly, as we drove for a while in silence. I could see her from the corner of my eye, constantly looking at me. I guess she was waiting for me to continue but wanted me to do it in my own time. I loved that about her. She was so patient.

"You know how I always told you that I never want to get hurt. Especially by someone else.. and now I'm hurt. And it's because of someone else. I just feel so stupid Hawa. I've always been so careful. And then he came. And out of nowhere, it felt like a miracle. But now? It feels nothing short of a punishment. I hate this feeling. At least with my mental health, I knew that even though my mind was in control; I could still help it. But this restlessness.. this pain in my heart.. I don't know. I don't know what to do." I said, looking at her as she parked the car and switched the engine off.

"I get you.. but what's happened? Because you told me you don't talk to him, and I know you would tell me if that changed?"

"Thats the thing Hawa.. we don't talk. Nothing has changed.. But my heart.. I just.. I don't know.. Am I being stupid?"

"No Dunya.. you're not being stupid. You're really not. Talk to me, vent.." She said, comfortingly.

I told her everything. From meeting him to praying for him to thinking of him with Saha.

"WHAT!? Where did she come from?" She said sounding annoyed.

131

"I don't know, but as I was leaving? I saw them talking, so there's that.."

"Wow.. I'm so sorry Dunya."

"See, I don't get what you're sorry about. Because there was nothing set in stone between us. If I was married to the guy, then fair enough it gives me a valid reason to be feeling jealous. To feel restless when I see him talking to anyone else.. but this is just a guy I've talked to a few times.."

"But it's more than that isn't it Dunya?" She said

"I don't want to though. I don't want to l.."

I stopped.

"I can't even bring myself to say it Hawa.. I'm so petrified. How long will this last?"

"Its not as easy as that though is it? You can't just say you don't feel a certain way and it changes like that. You still feel that way. This is a matter of your heart, and you know.. hearts never lie.. I know. I know you're scared because you believe you've been so careful. And I know you. You've never given someone the time of day, apart from me obviously You've always kept yourself to yourself. But with him.. it was different. You opened up, without even thinking twice. And I honestly, truly, believe there's more to this…"

"Hawa. I love you. But please don't give me hope. It hurts to have that hope for something I know won't happen.."

"But you don't know for certain do you? You think it because of what you've seen today. But we cant know everything right? Perhaps there's more to it than it seems?"

"I guess so.. But I need to carry on being careful. I need to stop praying for him. I need to stop seeing him around. I need to ignore him.."

"Don't do that to yourself Dunya. Why are you punishing yourself for something that isn't entirely in your control?"

"Because I want it to be in my control Hawa. I don't want to feel this way.."

"You can't stop that Dunya. You can't stop feelings. You've always told me to accept that what I feel. That if I avoid them; it wont make them go away. You can't expect something to be okay if you ignore it. There'll come a time when you feel it more than ever. And it'll hurt. More than it will if you just deal with it in that instance. I know you. And I know everything you've been through. I know that you can get through this. I know. Because you're so strong. Stronger than anyone I know.. So trust that this too will be okay. And don't worry so much about what you can't control. But just accept. Accept that there's certain feelings that are perfectly NORMAL to feel, and there's not much we can do apart from trust God. And know that whatever is happening? Is a part of His superior plan for you."

I sighed.

"You're right Hawa. I guess it'll take time."

"Definitely. Time reveals everything. So don't be disheartened with what's happening in this instance, and have faith that its Allah's plan and His plan always makes sense in the end."

We spent the rest of the day just going for a walk and talking about several things. I felt as though I needed it more than anything. And in the end, I felt a lot lighter. As though, this was the help my heart was seeking.

I went home that day, and I prayed. I prayed a lot.

"Ya Rab.." I began.

"Ya Rab. I know that now it's too late for me to ask of you to not attach my heart to anyone. I know that. But I also know. And I trust that there's more to this. So please make it make sense ya Rab. Ya Rab, allow to me to understand what this plan is. Allow me to live it. Ya Rab.. make it okay.. I know you will."

I always said this dua. At times, it would be the exact same words. And other times? I would say nothing more than "Ya Rab.. allow me to understand." I continued to pray Tahajjud, and it helped. Prayer always helped. It brought peace to the chaos. It brought sanity to my mind. And, I didn't feel so defeated when I was praying. I actually felt at peace. I actually felt okay. And it was through praying, that I realised. I realised that prayer is peace. Without prayer, I am nothing. Without prayer, I can do nothing. My heart needs prayer, the same way my body needs nutrients.

14

Second year of university had begun, and I promised myself a few things, before it had begun. I promised myself that I would try my best, but trying my best would also mean attending university as much as possible. That I couldn't put my education on hold for feelings. For my heart. That this is the success I know I deserved; and that I wouldn't acquire it if I constantly avoided it. So I promised myself to attend university as much as possible.

Winter was a weird season. At times, I found comfort in the early darkness, but most times, I hated it. I craved summer evenings, and late nights. I guess parts of winter constantly reminded me that darkness sometimes lingers for longer than it needs. But it's not soon until the sunrises again. Even on the darkest of days, there's hope. Even then.

It was 9AM and I always despised early morning lectures. Perhaps it was the early morning commute, and hating that everywhere was so busy. Or perhaps, the filled lecture theatres with everyone walking in with the scent of coffee following them. I don't what it was. But I didn't want to break my promise so soon. So I attended my 9AM lectures. All of them.

"Welcome back everyone! Today's lecture will be about your assignment.."

Great, an assignment already. But it wasn't just any assignment, it was a group project. And as you may know.. I wasn't so keen on them.

"So, have you got a group?" I heard a voice speak.

"Erm.. no.. I kind of don't talk to anyone so.." I said, as my cheeks started to burn up from becoming embarrassed.

"GIRL! It's okay. I'm the same, but hey, I'm Hannah. It's nice to meet someone similar to me for once." She said, smiling.

She seemed nice. I knew I couldn't paint her with the same paintbrush. I had a good feeling about her. She gave that sort of positive vibe you know?

"Room for one more?" It was him.

"Erm - isn't it meant to be groups of 3?" I was quick to reply.

He looked at me. And then to Hannah.

"I mean I may be bad at maths, but 1 + 1 equals 2, right?" He said sluggishly, as they both began to laugh.

"Yes, you can join." Hannah said.

I didn't know whether to be annoyed or overjoyed with happiness. I guess, a part of me was feeling both. It felt nice seeing him after so long. But we didn't really speak or see each other after the last time he saw me having a panic attack, and I still remember everything. And it's like when he's in front of me? I go blank. I don't feel control. I get happy. I get 'butterflies' as Hawa would say. But I didn't want to. I really didn't.

We spent the next hour after the lecture going through the assignment specification and talking about what we could include in the presentation. And at points, we would get silent. I would catch him looking at me, as though he wanted to change the topic, talk about something else. But I ignored it. I didn't want to get into this so soon into the year. I just wanted to move on from these feelings.

"Be right back guys, just gonna go get something to drink!" Hannah said, as she grabbed her purse and walked out the room.

"Great." I whispered to myself.

"Hey.. Dunya?" He was quick to speak.

I looked up at him. And paused for a second. There was something about him. He seemed different.. I mean not like I probably knew much about him anyways. But.. he just didn't seem himself. He seemed… tired.

"Yeah, bus boy?"

He smiled. "Musa. The name's Musa."

"I mean I prefer bus boy but okay." I said smirking.

"As you wish." He said smiling.

He then placed his book onto the table in front of him, and suddenly the feeling of seriousness filled the air.

"You okay?" I asked.. probably for the first time.

"Yeah.." He paused.

"Well.. no. That's kind of why I wanted to speak to you.." He looked down at his hands. He held them tightly together and kept shaking his legs. This seemed familiar.

"It's just. You're the only other person that I know that has gone through this, and I wanted to talk to you.." He said, sighing.

"You know how, the first time we spoke, you told me I was strong? I mean what I'm about to say won't make me seem strong.. but rather weak.."

"Hey.. don't say that. Remember you told me everyone that goes through mental health difficulties is strong, no matter how they might deal with them?" I said.

"You remember?" He asked, slightly smiling.

I smiled back and waited for him to continue.

He told me how he recently began to feel distant from religion. From Allah. He told me that he kept having these doubts. These thoughts that perhaps everyone in his life would be better off without. In all honesty? I found what he said, quite heavy to digest. But also relatable, because I had been through the same. I still had those days, where I felt 'weak'. I knew what it was like, having all these thoughts, all these overwhelming feelings, yet no-one in person to share them with. So, I wanted to help him. Always. But I also didn't want him to depend on me. I knew that, this kind of dependent should be only on Allah.

"You know that feeling like that doesn't make you weak right?"

"You think so?" He asked.

"I know so. And if anything, this is one of the things I'm most certain about Musa.. When I went through exactly what you're going through, one of my worst phases, I felt the same. I felt as though there was darkness wherever I turn. I tried to pray, I tried to connect to Allah, for a while and it just didn't help as much as I wanted it to. But then I stopped. I asked myself: how long am I going to do this for? How long am I willing to pray? And, most answers pointed towards 'temporary.' I felt as though

139

prayer is a temporary fix at the start, and I was wrong. I was wrong to think that. So I changed the way I thought of prayer. I didn't think of it as though its a burden. As though it's something I have to do.. I mean it is, of course it is obligatory, but I also told myself that it's something my soul needs. Something my heart needs. I can't turn to it with the intention that I'm only going to pray until I feel better. Because that would be wrong. Prayer is so much more than that, you know? I spent majority of my time, researching, reading into prayer. Making notes of the positives, the peace that comes with it. And I promised myself one thing.." I said.

"What was that?" He asked.

"I promised myself that I would pray regardless of what I felt. If I felt pain, and I needed to talk to Allah? I would pray. But if I felt content. And I felt as though I couldn't be happier in those moment? I would still pray. Because I learnt that nothing is set in stone. Neither happiness, nor darkness. Both feelings, both emotions flee from us as quickly as they come around. And the only feeling that remains? Is the feeling of contentment. The feeling that you are defeating your nafs. The feeling that you're not giving up, no matter how hard it is. You're not giving up, even if Allah has already responded to what you've asked for. You're not giving up, because He didn't give up on you."

"Wow." He said. Taking a minute to digest it.
"That's a beautiful way of thinking of it.. but.."

"I know.." I said.

"I know, there's a difference between hearing something and accepting it. There's a difference between knowing that something is right, but then fully accepting it. Applying it. But this is all a test. He knows. He knows that there will be times in our lives where we feel as though we can't go on. We can't go on pretending that it'll be okay, when we don't accept that it'll be okay. I guess for you, the hardest part is that you're finding it harder to convince yourself that happiness is near. You're finding it harder to accept the better possibilities. The ending to the tunnel doesn't seem as close as you may have made it out to be at the start. Perhaps, you're at that point in the tunnel where you're neither at the start, but neither towards the end. You're in the middle. Darkness before you, but also believing darkness is ahead.."

"How do you explain it so well?"

"I understand it too." I said.

"I feel that exact same way. But I just don't know what to move ahead. I don't want to be stuck in the middle forever you know?"

"Of course. No-one does. But I guess, it's when we're in the middle that we've gotta try the hardest. Think of it like this, when someone begins a business. At the start, they're eager. They're motivated. But then the not so busy days seep in, and they realise that nothing is easy as it seemed. They doubt their work and they doubt the possibilities of business ever picking up. But they want it to. So they try harder. They do what they can. Because deep down? They still have that tiny bit of faith, that it'll be a success. Similarly? Deep down, you have that feeling. You have that feeling you had when we first met. That it'll be okay. That you'll get through this. You still have that faith in yourself. That faith is not gone. It's just a matter of reminding yourself daily. Daily affirmations, you know?"

At this point, he was writing in his notepad. And then stopped, when I did. I didn't think much of it. I assume he was just doodling. I do that too sometimes.

"I really don't know how to thank you.. This has been so refreshing to hear. Thank you Dunya. Seriously." He said, looking at me. He caught my eye for a second, and we locked eyes again. But we were quick to look away.

I shrugged it off, as I usually do.

"It's okay.. in sha Allah it gets easier for you.." I said, picking up the textbook from the desk in front of me as a way of trying to get back to work.

"Yeah.. back to work.." Hannah said, as she creeped up behind us.

"Dunya is a wise one!" She said as she smiled.

How long had she been listening?

"Don't worry I wasn't eavesdropping. I just heard you talking about businesses, and you've convinced me. Hannah's boutique coming soon."

We all laughed away. She reminded me of Hawa in a lot of ways. She always brought humour into things, to try and lighten the mood.

"So, that's enough for today. I don't think my brain can hack anymore reading." Hannah said, as we all packed up and got ready to leave.

"I agree.." I said. Looking up at her and realising she was writing a note.

"Take this." She said, as she passed me her number.

"I mean I can't say I'm not in the slightest offended, but you girls do you." Musa said, laughing in the process.

I liked how he didn't ask. I liked how he didn't ask me for my socials. Or for my number. I preferred it that way. I guess, he was equally scared of attachments too. But, was I stupid for thinking in the slightest that he may feel these feelings too?

I went home that day and spoke to Hawa. I told her about the conversation I had with Musa, and she was eager to know what happened next. She kept asking for 'details'. I guess, she knew I was too scared to accept the reality, but we both knew.

I prayed for him again that night. And for the several nights to follow. I didn't know what else to do to help. It was the only way I knew, would help him. It was also the only thing I knew would help me. Help me come to terms with these feelings. I asked Allah for him.. but in a way that didn't cause hurt.

I wrote a lot too during that first semester. I saw him a lot because of the project we did, so I had no other way of dealing with the thoughts, the feelings.. but to write. So I wrote.

> "I'm a firm believer in the fact that prayer is the purest form of love.."

I paused. Wow. Love. Are you really calling it that Dunya? I guess.. it was.

> "I mean, what's more beautiful than talking to Allah, the knower of all hearts, about the residents of our hearts? There's just something about it. About talking to someone you love to Allah, and knowing that no matter what happens? Allah will protect them. It's like you're asking Allah to protect them more than anything. To look out for them. It's like you're asking Allah to take care of them.. until He unites you in a union so strong.. that you can take care of

143

them too. So I guess, I'll talk about him to Allah, and at least for now? I'll leave him in His care. I know that someday, Allah will help him to find himself. I know that he probably doesn't see it now. I know in this instance, the pain he carries within doesn't make sense. His mind's a blur and he has no sense of direction. But I'll ask Allah to guide him. I know it more than anyone, he's not lost for good, he'll find his way home. If anything, he just needs to seek the voice inside his heart, the one we often silence for way too long. I know that once he finds Allah, he'll find himself. I know. So I pray for him. And I'll continue to pray. That someday he finds Allah in the very pain he talks of today. And I pray that through this, he finds himself too."

I stopped. I kept reading over it. I still couldn't believe that this how I felt. Truth be told. I still felt very conflicted. Although, I knew now how I felt. I still felt guilty. As though there's something I'm doing wrong. As though I perhaps didn't protect myself enough. So sometimes? I sit and I ask nothing more from Allah but to protect me. To protect me from giving myself to the wrong one. But to also make him right for me. I had hope, mostly. But parts of me felt that I was perhaps hoping too much. And it was like an endless cycle. Of good days and bad. Of good feelings and bad.

I stuck to my promise. You know, the one where I promised to make the most of my education and to attend as many lectures as possible. In fact? I attended all my lectures in the first semester. At times? I would see Musa and I would purposely look the other way or sit far from him. But then other times? I would want him to sit near. I just wanted to know him. To talk to him.. But, I also didn't want to do something I know I would regret. So I did what I do best, and I continued to pray for him, whilst also hoping that these feelings weren't in vain.

The winter break was among us, and I couldn't think of anything better to do but to read. So I spent a lot of time doing that. I read into love in Islam. And I seemed more invested in love.. more than I had been before.

I wrote a lot more too.

> "Love. A part of my strongly believes that love that is written to be ours will never leave us wondering who we are. We won't leave us feeling a though we are lost. Love that is chosen by Him, will never leave us broken. It'll never leave us chasing things or people. It'll keep us content. It'll make us feel whole. We won't feel broken, we won't feel weak. Love written by God, is a love that is worth waiting for, because it's a love that'll turn our weaknesses to strength. True love is never meant to leave us feeling as though the weight of the whole world lives in our hearts - it'll make us feel free. Love isn't always a negative thing.."

I fell asleep that night, feeling content. I knew that Allah was answering my duas. That He was helping me cope with what I was feeling, because I kept finding these short bursts of inspiration through writing. I knew that He will allowing me to understand through guiding me to certain things. And researching love was one of those things.

There was no more assignments to do for a while, so I was looking forward to sleeping in later than usual. I fell asleep thinking about love. Thinking about what I felt. And I hoped that the start was near. But I also convinced myself that I shouldn't hope as much. Because perhaps it'll turn out completely different to how I want it to. And if it does? I shouldn't feel defeated, but thankful.. that Allah saved me.

15

"DUNYA, YOUR ALARM!!!!" I heard my brother screaming from outside my bedroom.

Yeah, he was totally going to be angry at me for the rest of the week. This wasn't the first time my alarm had woken him up before me.
I turned my alarm off and saw that it was already 10AM.
I didn't really have anywhere to go that day, so I was hoping to sleep in, but I guess I forgot to turn my alarm off last night.

I got dressed and began walking down the stairs. I stopped midway, because I saw shoes in the corridor, and heard voices coming from the living room.

"Bro?" I said, as I went back up and knocked on my brother's door. It was opened so I walked in.

"Seriously? Do you have a death wish today or?" He said, sounding as annoyed as ever.

"Okay.. but who's downstairs? At THIS time?"

"Some friends of Dad. I think they've come to ask for your proposal."

"WHAT!" I exclaimed at the top of my voice.

"Shhh!" He said, as he knocked lightly on the wall and said: "Thin walls Dunya!"

"They're downstairs, not in the other room idiot!" I said, sitting down on his chair and not having a care that he was annoyed.

He sat up in his bed, and just sighed, knowing full well that I wasn't going to let him sleep now.

"But who?" I said, trying not to sound so eager or interested.. because I really wasn't.

"Not sure, but apparently Mum's eager for you to say yes.."

"How do YOU know all this about MY life before I do?"

"I guess I'm just home more to listen to conversations."

"The cheek of it!" I laughed as I threw his cushion at him.

We sat there scrolling through our own phones for a few moments, before my phone began to ring. It was my Mum.

"Is it Mum?"

"Here, answer it for me, say I'm asleep!"

"And, why would I have YOUR phone?" He said, as I threw my phone towards him.

"Yeah mum? She's right here." He said, with the biggest smirk on his face. "Revenge" he whispered.

I looked at him and gave him a death stare, before walking out the room, holding the phone next to my ear.
"Yeah mum?" I asked, trying not to act like I knew.

"Can you get dressed and come down please?" She was whispering.

"Why are you whispering Mum?"

"There's some people here to see you. Just get dressed, and quickly come down." She didn't give me a chance to speak, as she cut the phone.

"Technically, she didn't say dress nice, so I can go down like this!" I said to myself.

I saw that my brother was stood shaking his head as he ran to block the staircase and pointed towards my room. Wow, he was eager to get rid of me, wasn't he?

I got changed and decided that I should perhaps make my 'entrance'. I just couldn't believe how strange this was. I didn't hear a peep from my parents about this so I was shocked as to why it seemed like this 'talk' had been going on for weeks.

I walked into the room and my jaw instantly dropped.
It was him. It was bus boy. It was Musa.

"Erm. Salaam.." I said trying not to stutter.

"There she is.." Said my Dad, as he walked towards me and pointed towards an empty seat.

This was possibly the most shocking, yet awkward times of my life. I had no idea what was going on or who they wanted me to marry. I just shook my head most times, and replied yes or no to their questions… almost felt like an interview.

I kept catching him looking at me. And then came the introduction.

"This is Musa.."

They explained how our parents were friends and were thinking about this proposal for a while. They knew we were both studying at the same university, doing the same course, and for them it only seemed like a match made in heaven.
I didn't know what to think at this point, I mean, was I dreaming? I swear, things like this only happen in movies? It felt surreal.
A few moments later, and then came the 'you two can talk to each other now' moment.

The rest of them left the room as we proceeded to sit in silence for a few seconds, before I couldn't keep my laughter in a second longer and began to laugh. But in those instances? I wanted nothing more than to pray to Allah and thank Him.

I could see that he was also trying so hard to keep his laughter in.

"Just let it out." I said, still laughing.

We laughed for a few moments, before I couldn't possibly laugh any more.

"This is.." He began to speak.

"Strange?" I asked.

"No.. well.. yeah.."

"I know that feeling!" I said.

He looked up at me and asked: "So.. did you feel it too?"

"Feel what?" I said, trying to be naive to the matter of fact that I knew what he was asking.

"As though, our meeting was nothing short of a miracle?"

I looked at him, and I smiled.
"I felt it too.. but.."

"But? That's never good.." He replied.

"I just have to ask.. is there someone else you have in mind? As in from university?" I said, clearly referring to Saha.

"Are you talking about that girl you saw me talking to? Honestly, that's nothing. She asked, and I told her I already have someone…"

My heart began to sink a little.

"Do you?" I had to know.

"Well, I do like someone. But it all depends on today, right?"

I looked down.

"Dunya? It's you." Musa said, with happiness beaming through his smile.

"Oh.."

"I mean, I knew I had to spell that out because you seemed to be a little upset?"

I began to smile. I raised my hand to cover my face and said:

"It's you, for me too.."

"Dunya.." He said, reaching out to hold my hand.

"You don't understand how happy that has made me. Honestly? Ever since I've met you, there's been something there. And I couldn't stop thinking about you. But I knew you were reserved. I had a feeling you were not keen on getting to know anyone. But it just felt so easy opening up to you, you know? It felt normal. As though, we might have met before. So I did what I had to do, and I asked Allah for you.." I began to cry.

He continued..

"Which is why when my parents spoke about someone named Dunya, I just had a feeling it was you, you know? And here we are.. I guess this really was meant to be.."

He looked at me, passing me a tissue and pointing towards my tears.

"Happy tears.." I said, smiling.

"I'm glad." He said, looking around the room as though he was searching for something.

He then proceeded to grab a sweet out of the glass jar and knelt down in front of me. I couldn't stop smiling at this point.

"So, Dunya, bus girl, will you marry me?" He asked as he held out the sweet ring and had the goofiest smile.

"Yes, bus boy, I will." I said, as I took the sweet… and ate it of course.

I still couldn't believe that this was happening. It felt like something straight out of a movie, and I did not expect it to happen so soon.. or even at all. I rushed to the prayer mat as soon as they had left. And I prayed to Allah. And I thanked Him. I knew that there was a reason as to why I was hoping so much, and Allah allowed me to see and live that reason. And for that I was so grateful.

"Dunya?" My mother spoke, as I was folding my prayer mat.

"Yes Ammi?"

"Sit down with me?" She asked.

"Yeah of course."

"I want to ask you something.."

I nodded my head, and awaited her question.

"Are you happy with this?"

She looked at me, as she continued.

"I know you. I know you would say yes, even if you weren't completely happy. But you would because you always put us first. But marriage isn't something small. It's your entire life.."

"Mum?" I said, as I reached out to her hand.

"I've met Musa before.."

"And?" She was quick to respond.

"We wouldn't really speak, apart from a couple of times.. But he seems really genuine. And one thing I've always told myself is that if there's anyone that wants best for me, other than Allah, it's my parents. My heart is somewhat agreeing with this. And I genuinely do feel happy.. Alhamdhulillah."

She pulled me into a hug and then passed my phone to me, and said: "I think you best tell Hawa before she gets mad at you for not saying anything."

"You know her too well!" I said, dialling her number.

"Hawa?"

"OH MY" she began to scream with happiness.

"Huh? What's gotten into you?"

"YOU SAID YES DIDN'T YOU?!"

"WHAT!? YOU KNEW?"

"Erm.. yes, I guess?" She said, laughing.

"Your mum told me and asked me if you had anyone else in mind.."

"HOW AWKWARD!" I exclaimed. But I couldn't help but laugh at the situation.

She began to talk about arrangements for the wedding. She always had a habit of planning way in advance, but I got her to come over rather than doing it all over the phone.

I met with Musa a few more times, and we would always Hawa with us.

"You know, I'm not getting married with you right?" She said, teasing us.

"Yes, but you're here for protection." I said, glancing over at Musa to see his reaction.

"Protection? I see.. I see how it is." He said, trying to look sad.

I couldn't help but laugh.

We planned the wedding together (with the help of Hawa of course), and we both agreed that it would be a small, intimate ceremony. The topic of finishing university came up often, but he always reassured me that his parents would allow me to continue studies after marriage. And that the rest would come after. It all felt like it was happening too fast at first, but I convinced myself that perhaps it was best for it to happen this way to prevent any unnecessary hurt. I guess the holidays were the perfect time to get married too, with no stress from university playing on our minds.

I was so adamant on having a small wedding, but one thing I promised my mum was that I would allow her to buy the dress I would wear, so we spent a lot of time shopping. Not that I'm complaining. You should know by now, how fond I am of shopping.. especially when I'm not the one paying.

"So?" I walked out from the dressing room and stood in front of my Hawa and Mum.

"How does it look?" I said, turning to face the mirror.

"WOW" Hawa said, all starry eyed.

"Ma sha Allah Dunya. This is it." She said, as I could tell she was about to tear up.

"Muuuuuum." I said, walking towards her.

"It's okay Aunty, you still have me, I'm not married yet.." Hawa said, trying to lighten the mood.

The next few weeks continued to become a bit of an emotional rollercoaster. This was usual, for any girl getting married. I would reminisce the memories I had in this house and we would often tear up talking about them as a family, but I knew, and they knew, that this was a part of growing up. And that I would make new memories with my in laws and husband.

Soon before we knew it, the day before the wedding was upon us, and my mother was busying herself with providing food to the guests. It wasn't a big wedding ceremony but we tried to do a little gathering before the wedding so that most of our relatives could feel a part of it. And at certain points, I would catch her eyes tearing up, but I knew that she was also happy for me. And she told me this several times. I guess I felt more nervous about leaving my family and beginning again, than anything else. But I also knew that this new chapter was something planned by Allah, and I had to trust that He knew best for me.

The day of the wedding was nothing short of a fairytale, and I felt a thousand emotions at once. But mostly? I felt happy. I felt content. And I felt at peace, knowing, that Musa was the one I was marrying.

16

<u>Present day:</u>

So I guess, there's the threads I had to pull from this mind off mine. And in a way, writing about this and talking about it, has helped me to realise a few things.

o Mental health is an ongoing battle
o I mustn't give up, Allah's help is not far off
o I will get through this, because I've got the strength to do so
o I'm not alone

I had a sudden burst of inspiration, so I got my notepad and began to write.

> "To be honest, I feel as though a lot of young people go through the same that I do. The truth is, everyone has mental health. But not everyone has a healthy mental health. I feel like it's something we have to realise: our mental health matters just as much as our physical health. We must take care of it the same way we take care of our bodies. Something I've learnt is that our mind is meant to be a positive place, but that's not always possible. It's not even realistic. It's not realistic to feel so positive and happy all the time. Because that's not a realistic picture of how life is. Some days we'll feel as though the whole is weighing us down and as though we aren't able to comprehend what it is that makes us feel so low, and somedays, we'll feel so happy.. so happy that we won't even remember what it felt like to feel so low. But on both these days, our minds are strong. They always were. Sometimes, we just have to convince ourselves of it."

"Are you writing again?" Musa said, as he came and sat next to me.

"You know it.." I said, looking up at him, smiling.
"You know Dunya?"

"Yeah?" I stopped.

"Sometimes, I get scared. I wonder if I'm not making you happy enough, which is why you feel the need to write so much.. I get insecure.. but then.. I read what you write, and it convinces me of one thing for sure.."

"And what's that?" I said, placing my notebook on the bed and reaching out for his hand.

"It's the fact that you are the most inspiring person I have ever met, and I wouldn't change you for the world."

At this point, I nudged him as to get him to stop as I was blushing enough already.

"No really, Dunya." He held both my hands, and looked at me.

"The first time we talked about all this.. our mental health, I didn't expect to feel so understood. I didn't expect someone to understand. But you did. No questions asked. No judgements passed. You listened. And I feel like that's what a lot of people need. A listener? And you listened to everything. Even the words I couldn't say, but it's as though your eyes read through the barriers I was trying so hard to keep up. I could tell, the first time you ever spoke, you were genuine. You always are. Every word you write? It heals. And I get it, I tell myself to stop thinking so negative. Because I get it. I get that you have to write because it heals you, but at the same time? You're healing me, and I know that, whoever reads your words.. it'll heal them too. I have faith."

At this point I was trying my best not to bawl my eyes out and I just clinged onto him.

It's crazy. I was always so adamant that I would never attach myself to anyone. I convinced myself that no human or no worldly thing deserved that kind of love. But then I met him. And I understood what it meant to love. But it wasn't the type of love that would hurt. It's the type of love that would uplift you. The type that would support you. I guess that's why love for the sake of Allah is the purest. It really is. And I learnt that through Musa.

Yeah, you guessed right. I wrote.

"Love. Truth be told, I stand by everything I've ever said about love. But now? I'm living it. I understand it. I understand what it means to love. To love without feeling as though there's more negativity than positivity. I genuinely feel as though love received through Allah, is the best love there could be. I learnt that when I married Musa. There isn't enough words possible to explain just what this feels like. But one thing is for certain, and it's that, love doesn't need to be negative. Love can be positive too. Loving someone other than Allah is okay. Because most times? Both of you are in this union, that completes you, but at the same time you know. You know without Allah, you wouldn't complete each other. And you help each other. To become the best versions of yourselves. To become the best you can. Because you don't want this love to end here on this dunya. You want it to continue, into the life that matters.. the eternal Hereafter."

To be honest, even though I was the happiest I had been in a long time, I also knew that it was naive of me to think that I'll always be happy, you know? I mean, I still had days where I didn't feel as good. Musa still had those days too. The only difference is that we would both try to help each other as much as possible, but we both knew that the Ultimate Healer is Allah. So we continued to turn to Allah, and we continued to fight the bad days.. with the help of Allah. We always talked about how mental health isn't something that leaves you, and that it's okay if some days we feel as though we are back to where we once were. But the reality is that we need to convince ourselves that we will never go back there. Because we've come so far from what we used to be, that we have shaped ourselves into stronger, more positive beings. And bad days will always occur. The only difference is? That we have gained the strength to fight back, and not give up.

The days when I feel closest to Allah, are the days He calls me towards Him and gives me the strength to respond. Not just once, but five times. A few years ago, many times, I used to think it was impossible. To pray five times. I didn't think I was capable. And I realise now, looking back, how empty my words were whilst praying. I would pray, but I wouldn't do it with full faith. So at times, when I would pray? I would ask Allah to have Mercy on this lost soul of mine. So, Allah sent me trials. And through those trials? He strengthened me. I continued to pray. And I still do. But the only difference? Every time I go to Him now, I place my heart in the palm of my hands and I ask Him to take it. I ask of Him to take my heart away from the dunya, and to allow me to continue placing it in front of Him.. The thing is, I've realised. I've realised how the prayer mat is my only safe place. And being in front of God no longer feels like something I need to do, but something my soul longs for. Something I long for. There's always this voice within me, begging, pleading, to go to that prayer mat, and talk to Allah. And for that I'm so thankful. For that very reason, I've learnt not to complain about my losses, but thank Allah instead. Had He not tested me, I would never have gained the strength to realise that without Him, there's no peace. Without prayer? There's no peace. Alhamdhulillah.

So I guess this is it. The last chapter of this journey. I have loads more to write. A lot more to say, but I pray that whoever reads this, understands that this pain? It's temporary. And once we reach the doors of Jannah, we'll get it. We'll understand why the dunya was the way it is. We'll understand why it was so hard at times. Once we reach Jannah, we'll realise.. it was worth it. It always was. It's going to be okay, even if it feels like it won't. It will be okay. You'll see.

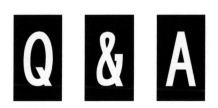

'Others tell me to be patient but surely it's easier said than done?'

"Of course. I don't think there's ever a "right" way to be patient. I feel like everyone is patient in their own ways. Some people show patience through holding their tears and anger in front of others. Some people show patience through praying. And some show patience by dealing with things privately. For me? Patience has always been about acceptance. Accepting that it's all a part of His plan. I learnt to accept that life was never meant to be perfect. There was always going to be trials. But these trials are always sent with a purpose. You see, Allah knows all that our heart contains. He knows that of which we don't even find the courage to speak. And He knows that the pain we feel like has no ending, really does. He knows that it's temporary. And He's sent it to us as a way to get us to reach out to what He has decreed. So, at times when we get lost in things that aren't entirely good for us and our souls, we begin to feel pain. But that pain is there for a reason. It's there to help us retrace our steps, and finally end up back where we were always intended to be: in front of Him. So when Allah tells us to be patient, it's because He knows just how close we are to overcoming these hurdles. He see's how close we are to the end. So, we have to accept that He wants best for us more than we have ever wanted best for ourselves. Trust that the One that created this heart of yours, is also the One that will heal it. Trust that He will get you through this, because He will.. Trust Him and that in itself is patience."

'Do you think it's true that Allah SWT takes away people that perhaps don't "deserve" you?'

"In simple terms.. yes. I've come to understand that whatever Allah tests us with is because He knows best for us, more than we can ever know best for ourselves. So sometimes, when we get attached to temporary people, and end up growing close to them and giving them our love and affection.. we believe we know what their intentions are, because of how close we've grown. But that's not always the case. The only One that knows the intentions of the heart, is the one that granted us the ability to love. He's the only One that knows what others intentions are with us. Therefore, when we suddenly grow apart from certain people, or we suddenly feel as though things aren't that great with them.. it's as though Allah is giving us a sign. A sign to perhaps leave those people where they are, because they've served their purpose in our lives. And most times, it leads to hurt. To pain. And majority of that pain is there to make us realise.. to help us learn not to pour so much into others when we don't know for sure what their intentions could be. I guess it's one of the reasons for why we've been told not to focus so much on temporary things, including people. Because Allah knows it can lead to hurt. So everything that He does, all the people He removes from our lives? It's for the better of our hearts."

'Why does it hurt so much when we expect from others?'

"I've learnt the hard way; that expecting from others isn't always something that's in your control. At the start, I used to expect a lot from certain people, and when they didn't meet my expectations, it broke me. I was in this state of denial that perhaps it's not my fault and it's entirely on them, for so long. And a part of it was on them. But then the blame game began, and I started to find faults in myself. I asked myself, how can I expect so much from this world? How can I expect myself to do so and not get hurt? It's not a fairytale right? It's real life. Truth is, every time we expect from others, we're putting our hearts at risk. We're risking ourselves getting hurt. We're allowing ourselves to be vulnerable. We're opening up a whole jar of possible scenarios and we're hoping for the best. But, the truth is, not everyone is capable of meeting your expectations. That's okay though. It's okay to expect. It's kinda human too, right? I've learnt that sometimes we expect so much because we're willing to do that much for them. We know how pure our intentions are and how sincere we are in our actions, and we see the world that way. We see the world through this lens of kindness, but not everyone's heart is the same as the one you hold. It's like we're so naive, we're basically just expecting things to be reciprocated. But, there comes a time where we have to accept the harsh fact that this is not always possible. Sometimes? People take more than they can give. And it's not your fault. So don't blame yourself. But just remind yourself to be careful. Remind yourself that any expectations from this dunya or it's people, are bound to let you down. The only One that won't, is Allah. I guess it's why it's called the testing place."

'How do I forgive and forget?'

"I often think about how people forgive those who have hurt them. Do they actually forgive them and how does this burden not remain? They say that when you forgive yourself, you're unburdening yourself of the pain you feel, and I used to think, how is that so? I always told myself that it's better to forgive than forget, because hearts have a stubborn nature and they seem to latch onto the things that once made them feel whole. But, it came to a point where I had to convince myself: I'm only going to heal if I forgive. Forgiving doesn't mean you want them back. It doesn't mean you want some form of contact or that you would give it another try. Forgiving means letting something that has had such a big hold over you for so long.. finally go. It's like setting it free. Majority of the time, when someone hurts us we become so defensive or hurt, that in turn it makes us bitter about certain situations. But that bitterness is there because you haven't forgiven them. Forgiving them does more good to you than it does to them. You're worthy of living without that burden. You don't need them or the memory of them tying you down more than it already has. Don't get me wrong, forgiving someone doesn't happen overnight. It's not an "okay I forgive you" process and magically you've forgiven them. It takes a hell of a lot to forgive them. But it's for YOU. This forgiveness is for YOU. So that YOU can move on. So that YOU can have the happiness that you deserve. So knowing this and keeping this as a reminder every time you feel yourself regretting ever thinking about forgiving them - is what will help you to forgive. You deserve this forgiveness more than they do. Do it for you. Do it for your heart. It'll take time, but keep in mind how beautiful it'll feel to have a mind that doesn't hold negative people there."

'Is it possible to love again after your heart has been broken?'

"I believe that love is something that doesn't leave you as easily as you may think it does. Sometimes we think that love is defined by the length of time we've known someone, or perhaps defined by the sacrifices we've made to achieve their love. But love is much more. And when hearts break, love doesn't. You become distant with the person, or cut them from your life, but the love is still there. Love is not an emotion, but a life long connection. As much as we might hate to accept it, love will always be there. It doesn't have to be a bad thing though. You see we meet several people in our lives, we fall for some and they become difficult to forget. It's because although they are absent from our lives, they still live on in our hearts. It's okay though. I guess, a part of moving on, is accepting that this is the case. That your past is still a part of you, no matter how hard you try to paint over it. So, I guess, love is possible. More than once. I say this because I truly believe that sometimes we have to experience a love that isn't written for us, just so that we can come to know the worth of love when it is actually written for us. I feel like, when we break once, we stop looking for love. But that's when love comes looking for us. We forget that we don't always need to chase after what has already been written, because Allah will provide us with it at a time when we are emotionally ready to receive it. Only He knows when that is. But don't give up on love, just because of one bad experience. You never know what the future holds. Only He knows. Have trust in His plan, and know that He has promised you ease after hardship."

'How do I stop comparing my life to others?'

"Everyone walks towards the same things, but there's different timings for everything. It's so easy to look to social media and see that certain people are getting things before you, but the more you compare the more you'll feel insecure about your life. Your life is going exactly the way Allah has planned it. What's not to say that those people you constantly compare with have already been through what you're going through right now? You see you cannot know someones entire story - just what they show you - just what you see as the outsider looking in. Everyone has the same start and same ending: from Allah to Allah, but how you are in the middle, depends completely on how Allah has written it to be. So it might be that Allah has planned for you to marry later than all your friends, or that He's planned for you to finish your education way after your friends - but that doesn't make you any less important. It shouldn't affect the way you see your life. It's okay if your friends or those around you are living their life differently, because that's their journey and you are not aware of what they had to go through to get there. Just like, Allah is making you wait, for you to get what you want. You cannot spend your life comparing every little thing, because your life is so much different to anyone else. Allah has taken so much consideration into planning your life, making it as best as possible for you, making sure happiness is written for you, so it's okay if it's not the same as your friends: it was never written to be the same. You are different and that's okay, because we are all made to be different. Everyone walks towards the same direction, but the path you walk isn't always the same. And that's okay. Because whatever path you are written to walk, is written for you for a certain reason; because it's best for you."

'How do you accept that God's plan is the best plan?'

"Sometimes when we're going through a tough trial, we think so negative about the future too. I guess, it's normal. You're bound to think negative when negativity is surrounding you. You think about all that could go wrong, but never that everything could actually be okay. Sometimes, people call that "too hopeful." And it's that hope that scares you because you don't know, you're uncertain about the future because you don't know what new trials it'll bring. And that's completely normal. Truth is, we don't know what will happen in the next few minutes, so how can we possibly guess what'll happen in the next few months or years? We can hope, because that hope is there for a reason. But the most important thing that helps - is trusting Allah. It's knowing that He loves you more than love itself. It's knowing that He created you in the most perfect version of you. He created the cells that live within you, and the heart that resides within. He created you with such perfection; so of course your future is also in safe hands. He has planned the next thing you'll do after you read this, He's planned the number of breaths you'll take within each minute, and He's planned what'll happen in the next few years. He has planned it all, down to every little detail. But, we don't know what the detail is. We take the little things that surround the detail and we try to make sense of it all, but we can't. We're simply human. His wisdom is such that we cannot begin to comprehend. He knows, He knows what is best and when it's best for us to have it. It might take a while for to realise, but once we do, we'll come to understand why His plan is the best plan. It's the most freeing feeling in the world, knowing that your fate is in the hands of the One that loves you more than anything. And I pray that we all experience this feeling."

'How do I let go of my past?'

"I'll be honest, this isn't easy. Just like any other trial, this is also a difficult one. But what makes it easier is accepting it. You have to accept the past for what it was. For what you've been through. For what it's taught you. You have to accept that perhaps certain things had to happen. But it doesn't stop there. This is where you need to remind yourself to have Tawakkul. This is where you remind yourself that Allah has so intricately planned every little detail in your life. To what time you wake up and what you choose to eat, to who you are as an individual in the future. It's all decided. It's all written. Think of it like this: when you're reading a book, or watching a movie, you often think about the ending and how it'll end and get carried away with what things could occur rather than what has already been, right? Because who even chooses to focus on the past? But the past isn't all bad. Yes, it's hurt. Yes, you'd rather forget it. But you wouldn't be here right now, if it wasn't for your past. You are the person you are because of it. And you will become the person that Allah has written you to be, because of it. So, no matter how bitter, no matter how heartbreaking, start by accepting it. Accept your past for what it was and know that there was good in it. Even if you cannot seem to view it in a positive light right now, you will soon enough. Sometimes, we have to accept what once was, just so that we can allow ourselves to move forward and begin to accept better things too."

'Does praying for someone you love, bring them back?'

"I've always believed that when you're on the prayer mat? It's when your heart feels most at home. It's when you feel most at home. You tend to speak about things you can't speak to anyone else about. You admit things to Allah and you speak to Him, as though you are certain He is listening. And you have full faith that He hears you. I've learnt that this is why we always leave the prayer mat feeling somewhat at ease, you know? So when you pray for the ones you love; the ones that have left - the calling to pray for them doesn't always mean you want them back. Sometimes it means that they are in need of prayers. Sometimes it means that Allah has placed someone like you in their lives so that they receive prayers. So that they receive heartwarming duas. You see, when we lose people we love: we imagine how it'd be for them to come back. And that's completely normal. I guess? In these situations, you've just gotta keep praying. Only Allah knows what is planned for you. And it could be that by praying for them, they do return. Or it could be that by praying more and more: you're becoming closer to Allah. And in both situations? Your heart will be at ease. Because you're praying. You know that your fate lies with Allah, and you're placing your hopes in Him. And that's all that matters. Because He will reveal what is right for you, when you are ready to receive it. Keep praying. Keep trusting Him. His plans won't let you down. He won't let you down."

'How to pray for the ones that broke us?'

"I used to often wonder how it was possible for people to forgive others so easily. I used to think how it was even possible for others to proudly say that even though someone hurt them.. they still pray for them. I didn't think of it as realistic. I didn't think any sane person would pray for someone when that person has hurt them. But then I got hurt. I got hurt by the same people I would pray for. And some may say that I perhaps just stopped being naive. But, I just understood more. A lot more. I came to learn that sometimes people hurt us and yet our hearts have this habit of clinging onto them. So it directs towards them at times when we feel most vulnerable: including the prayer mat. And I guess? More than anything it shows that we are stronger than the negativity that tries to make us turn cold. I've always believed that forgiving someone takes a lot of strength and prayer is one of the most beautiful ways of forgiving someone. It's accepting that you couldn't control their actions - but you can control your own. It's accepting that there's just so much you can control when it comes to others. It's accepting that it's okay. It's okay if you don't have complete control over what happens to you. Or over what hurts you. It's okay because not everything can be controlled. I came to understand that perhaps praying for them is my outlet. The only way to release the hurt they caused me. I came to learn that perhaps they're in need of prayers. That perhaps Allah has given me the chance to pray for them.. so that they may be saved by the hurt they cause their own souls. So I pray. I pray for them, and at the same time? I hope. I hope that these prayers are the reason for why their hearts are not turned to stone.."

QUOTES

And that's the beauty in trusting in

Allah's timing.

You come to believe that He wants

best for you,

more than

you've ever wanted best for yourself.

And so,

I told myself:

"My heart is not safe

in this dunya

unless it's with Allah."

A heart
isn't a home
unless Allah
has entered it.

And then,

there's some conversations

that I save

just for the prayer mat.

It's because I've learnt that:

Allah provides the kind of comfort

that humans cannot.

READ THIS QUR'AN VERSE WHEN...

You're feeling...

o Upset: 3:159 / 3:139

o Anxious: 8:30 / 2:45

o Weak: 4:28

o Distant from Allah: 13:28

o Losing patience: 55:60 / 6:71 /64:11

o Unappreciated: 76:22

o Sinful: 39:55

o Tired of trials: 94:05

The Qur'an is the ultimate healer,
for surely nothing warms our hearts more than
listening to the words of Our Creator.

Dua - For anxiety and sorrow

اللَّهُمَّ إِنِّي عَبْدُكَ، ابْنُ عَبْدِكَ، ابْنُ أَمَتِكَ، نَاصِيَتِي بِيَدِكَ، مَاضٍ فِيَّ حُكْمُكَ، عَدْلٌ فِيَّ قَضَاؤُكَ، أَسْأَلُكَ بِكُلِّ اسْمٍ هُوَ لَكَ، سَمَّيْتَ بِهِ نَفْسَكَ، أَوْ أَنْزَلْتَهُ فِي كِتَابِكَ، أَوْ عَلَّمْتَهُ أَحَداً مِنْ خَلْقِكَ، أَوِ اسْتَأْثَرْتَ بِهِ فِي عِلْمِ الْغَيْبِ عِنْدَكَ، أَنْ تَجْعَلَ الْقُرْآنَ رَبِيعَ قَلْبِي، وَنُورَ صَدْرِي، وجَلَاءَ حُزْنِي وذَهَابَ هَمِّي

120. Allaahumma 'innee 'abduka, ibnu 'abdika, ibnu 'amatika, naasiyatee biyadika, maadhin fiyya hukmuka, 'adlun fiyya qadhaa'uka, 'as'aluka bikulli ismin huwa laka, sammayta bihi nafsaka, 'aw 'anzaltahu fee kitaabika, 'aw 'allamtahu 'ahadan min khalqika, 'awista'tharta bihi fee 'ilmil-ghaybi 'indaka, 'an taj'alal-Qur'aana rabee'a qalbee, wa noora sadree, wa jalaa'a huznee, wa thahaaba hammee .

120. O Allah, I am Your slave and the son of Your male slave and the son of your female slave. My forehead is in Your Hand (i.e. You have control over me). Your Judgment upon me is assured and Your Decree concerning me is just. I ask You by every Name that You have named Yourself with, revealed in Your Book, taught any one of Your creation or kept unto Yourself in the knowledge of the unseen that is with You, to make the Qur'an the spring of my heart, and the light of my chest, the banisher of my sadness and the reliever of my distress. [Ahmad 1/391]

Dua - For anxiety and sorrow

اللَّهُمَّ إِنِّي أَعْوذُ بِكَ مِنَ الـهَمِّ وَ الْحَـزَنِ، وَالعَجْـزِ وَالْكَسَـلِ، والبُخْـلِ والْجُبْنِ، وضَلَعِ الدَّيْنِ وغَلَبَةِ الرِّجَالِ

121. Allaahumma 'innee 'a'oothu bika minal-hammi walhazani, wal'ajzi walkasali, walbukhli waljubni, wa dhala'id-dayni wa ghalabatir-rijaal.

121. O Allah, I seek refuge in you from grief and sadness, from weakness and from laziness, from miserliness and from cowardice, from being overcome by debt and overpowered by men.

[Al-Bukhari 7/158]

Dua - For those in distress

اللَّهُمَّ رَحْمَتَكَ أَرْجُو فَلَا تَكِلْنِي إِلَى نَفْسِي طَرْفَةَ عَيْنٍ، وَأَصْلِحْ لِي شَأْنِي كُلَّهُ، لَا إِلَهَ إِلَّا أَنْتَ

123. Allaahumma rahmataka 'arjoo falaa takilnee 'ilaa nafsee tarfata 'aynin, wa 'aslih lee sha'nee kullahu, laa'ilaaha 'illaa 'Anta.

123. O Allah, I hope for Your mercy. Do not leave me to myself even for the blinking of an eye. Correct all of my affairs for me. There is none worthy of worship but You.

[Ahmad 5/42]

Thank you for reading

I pray that this book has given you some insight into things you may struggle with. I pray that it has helped you in some form or another. I pray that you've learnt at least one thing.
May Allah protect you always. Ameen ♡

- lostinthedunya

Printed in Great Britain
by Amazon

78935247R00104